RHYTHM and ROLE PLAY

plays by

CAROLYN GRAHAM

cartoons by

SERGIO ARAGONES

edited, and with procedures by

JOAN ASHKENAS

JAG PUBLICATIONS

Acknowledgment

I'd like to express thanks to my editor, Joan Ashkenas, for initiating the original idea for this book and for inviting me to be a part of it. Her support, encouragement and creative input have brought this project to life.

— Carolyn Graham

Published by JAG Publications
11288 Ventura Blvd.
Studio City, CA 91604
(818) 505-9002

Design by Words & Deeds

Library of Congress Catalogue Card Number 91-060279

Printed in the United States of America

ISBN 0-943327-08-3

10 9 8 7 6 5 4 3 2 1

Contents

Introduction

What is *Rhythm and Role Play?*

Humor is the foundation of this multi-faceted text. Promoting natural language is its function. Each unit begins with a witty, uncaptioned sequential cartoon story. This is followed with a rhythmic play based on the cartoon. In each play, all students in the class are involved. There are individual roles for two or three characters, and a chorus for all the others. Exercises that follow relate to listening, discussion and writing. In other words, students have opportunities to internalize the new language and expressions they have learned in a particular context. They are offered both structured and creative, improvisational activities.

Suggested Procedures for Introducing the Cartoon Stories

Low Intermediate Level

Start by helping students identify vocabulary items in the story. You say a word, the class repeats it. You write it on the blackboard, the class writes it on their cartoons. Name as many things as you can, moving ahead one frame at a time. When students have learned this vocabulary, go back and help them with descriptive phrases or dialogue. Again, you say it, they repeat it, you write it on the board, they write it. In this way, they gain the vocabulary to tell the story, frame by frame. After this, you might have them form small groups, students each taking a turn telling the others about a single frame, until all have had an opportunity to speak.

Working alone or with a partner, have students study the cartoon and answer the following questions:

Who are the main characters?

What does each one want?

What is the problem?

Where is the action taking place?

Pick one student to choose pairs around the class. Have each pair write one question about the story and put it in a hat. Pass the hat. Partners help each other answering the questions.

Create a name for the cartoon. Have students choose a name that will attract the interest of the readers and make them want to read it.

Let students look over the Table of Contents and choose which story title they wish to read first. Which attracts their attention, and why?

Intermediate and Advanced Levels

These cartoons work well for paired activities. You might have Students A open their books, look at the story and tell it to Students B. Then, Students B must retell it to their partners before actually seeing it. The challenge for Students A is in describing as clearly as possible the sequence of events. A more difficult variation of this is for one student to tell the story to the entire class, who must ask as many questions as they can. After, they must write the story.

A major benefit of these uncaptioned cartoons, both for oral and written work, is that students do not need to invent a story plot. Each cartoon is complete, with a "punch line." But the students' creativity comes into play as they tell it in their own words, and at their individual levels of proficiency. You may want to have them write descriptive pieces, or short plays with dialogue.

As oral improvisations, students might enjoy having a class member choose, or cast, certain fellow students in the individual roles. It is both interesting and fun if casting is done completely without regard to the sex or age of the student-actor. Perhaps an older man could be a baby, or a young girl student, a cave man. These actors should be encouraged to dramatize freely, with gestures, nods and grimaces to convey extra meaning. Then perhaps the next day a second improvisation could be enacted with a different casting director and different actors. Or they may enjoy a more formal presentation by gathering in groups and deciding beforehand what the characters will say.

There are enough plays and characters so that over a period of time everyone should have a chance to be an actor.

Development of communicative skills is the main concern here. But, unless there is a real problem in understanding a student's pronunciation or meaning, it is suggested that spontaneity be encouraged and that corrections of usage or pronunciation be left for a later time.

Suggested Procedures for Presenting the Plays

Initially the class reads along silently while listening to the entire play. For a second reading, the instructor could say each line, and the students repeat it. Appropriate stress and intonation will clarify and enhance meaning. By this time, much of the vocabulary will have been learned from the cartoon stories. Please be aware that the plays do not always follow those cartoons exactly, but sometimes depart from them with a different twist. For example, you might find a female character in the play where there was a male in the cartoon. Or perhaps an ending is changed slightly, or amplified. Obviously, it is important that students understand the meaning of any new vocabulary before enacting the plays.

You will find that the dialogues are written in conversational, informal style. Many current expressions are used, some of which may not be used by every native English speaker. Consequently, students will learn some idiomatic expressions that are used often in the street, on television, or in the movies, but not necessarily in formal writing for the classroom.

The combination of rhythm and repetition promotes an easy flow between words, encouraging pronunciation and phrasing as in normal conversation.

The exercises follow the plays. Ask Your Partner is found in all units. It is for discussion first, followed by writing. The suggested procedure is for it to be a paired activity. However, if that is not possible, it could also be done as an individual exercise, or even as a class exercise. The other oral exercise found in some units is Words and Expressions. Many common American expressions and sayings listed here undoubtedly will find comparison with those of other languages. Ideally, this will lead to some interesting class discussion. There are three types of word puzzles scattered throughout. For them, an answer key is at the back of the book.

A major and salutory attribute of role-playing is that students have fewer inhibitions when being "someone else." Humor allows them to relax, and enjoyment is part of the process of learning.

A personal comment: I feel privileged to have contributed to *Rhythm and Role Play,* both as editor and by writing some of the exercises. It has been a real pleasure to work with Carolyn Graham, whose spontaneity, humor and enthusiasm radiate from every page.

— Joan Ashkenas, Editor

6

THE TALKING WATCHDOG

CAST OF CHARACTERS

BURGLAR
TALKING WATCHDOG
CHORUS

Chorus Sound asleep, the street is asleep,
Sound asleep, asleep like a log.
The street is asleep, sound asleep,
Not a mouse, not a cat, not a bird,
Not a dog.

Burglar Ah, an open window!
I hope nobody's home.
A nice open window,
I hope nobody's home.

Chorus Nobody's home.
Nobody's home.
Open the window
and climb right in.

Burglar What's that thing on the floor?
It looks like a bunch of socks.
Dirty socks, it must be socks.
It must be a bunch of socks.

Chorus Dirty socks,
Dirty socks,
It looks like a pile of socks.

Dog Dirty socks! Listen to that!
I'm not a pile of dirty socks.
I'm a dog, woof, woof.
I'm a talking dog.
I'm a great big beautiful talking dog.

Chorus He's a dog, woof, woof.
He's a talking dog.
He's a great big beautiful talking dog.

Burglar Just my luck!
A talking dog.
That's what I need!
A talking dog!

Chorus Just his luck,
Bad luck,
A great big loud-mouthed
talking dog.

Burglar SH! Nice dog.
Be quiet, good dog.
I'm glad I brought this steak.
Sit! Sit!
Don't make noise.
Don't make noise.
Sh! Sh! Be a good dog.
Sh! Sh! Be a nice dog.

Burglar Oh boy, oh boy, oh boy, oh boy!
Look at this! Look at that!

Dog Mister, hey!

Burglar What did you say?

Dog Where's my steak?

Burglar Your what?

Dog My steak, my steak.

Burglar I gave you your steak.
You ate it.

Dog Where's the other one?

Burglar What other one?

Dog The other one, the other one,
Where's the other one?

Burglar There IS no other one.

Dog You only brought ONE?
That's no fun.

Burglar I only brought one.

Chorus He only brought one,
He only brought one,
That's no fun.

Dog ONE steak,
One little steak.

Burglar Don't get excited,
Please be quiet.
You'll wake up the neighbors.
Please calm down.

Dog I want steak,
and I want it now.

Burglar I'll bring it later.

Dog I want it now.

Burglar I'll bring it tomorrow.

Dog I want it now.
Right now.

Chorus Not later, right now.
Not tomorrow, right now.

Dog I know what I want
and I want it now.

Chorus He knows what he wants
and he wants it now.

Chorus What do you want?

Dog Steak!

Chorus When do you want it?

Dog Now!

(Dog continues to bark and wake up the neighbors. The burglar leaps out the window and runs away).

Burglar The street was asleep,
Asleep like a log,
and what did I get?
a talking dog!

The Talking Watchdog Exercises

Ask Your Partner

A. Ask your partner the following questions. Check the answers in the space provided.

	Yes	No
1. Does your mother like dogs?	☐	☐
2. Do people in your country keep watchdogs?	☐	☐
3. Would you like to be a professional dog trainer?	☐	☐
4. Does your landlord allow dogs in the building?	☐	☐
5. Do you think that a dog's life is easy?	☐	☐
6. Are dogs more difficult to take care of than cats?	☐	☐
7. Have you ever been robbed?	☐	☐
8. Do people always lock their doors at night in your country?	☐	☐

9. If you were a dog, would you prefer to be
   a. a big nervous watchdog ☐
   b. a fat, happy housedog ☐
   c. a smart hunting dog ☐
   d. a slim racing Greyhound ☐
10. Which of the following sounds would disturb you at night?
   a. a barking dog ☐
   b. a crying baby ☐
   c. a howling cat ☐

B. Write your own answers to questions 1-8 using a short response followed by a complete sentence.
Example: Do you like dogs? Yes. I do like dogs. I like dogs very much.

1. ________________. ________________.
2. ________________. ________________.
3. ________________. ________________.
4. ________________. ________________.
5. ________________. ________________.
6. ________________. ________________.

7. ______________________________. ______________________________.
8. ______________________________. ______________________________.

Pronunciation Practice

A. What's that thing?
B. What thing?
A. That thing on the floor. It looks like a ring.
B. A ring? That thing on the floor near the door?
A. That's right. Pick it up. I think it's a ring.

A. What are those things?
B. What things?
A. Those things on the floor. They look like rings.
B. Rings? Those things on the floor near the door?
A. That's right, pick them up. I think they're rings.

A. WHO is the watchdog watching?
B. The watchdog's watching YOU.
A. But WHO'S watching the watchdog?
B. I really wish I knew.
A. I wonder who's watching the watchdog.
B. Nobody's watching the watchdog.
A. Who is the watchdog watching?
B. The watchdog's watching YOU.

Words And Expressions

Sick as as dog	He's very sick
Works like a dog	He works very hard
Dog-tired	Very tired
Dog-eared	Pages turned down in a book
Puppy love	Young love
Dog eat dog	Very competitive
Doggie bag	Wrapped portion of food to take home from a restaurant
Dog days	Very hot, lazy days

In the dog house	In trouble
His bark is worse than his bite	He sounds tougher than he really is
They fight like cats and dogs	They fight all the time
Let sleeping dogs lie	Don't start trouble
Dog bites man—that's not news.	
Man bites dog—that's news.	

Word Search

How many words can you find?

In the puzzle below, find words from the story and circle them. Some go across, others go down.

Work with a partner. How many other words can you find that are not in the story? List all the words you can find on a separate piece of paper, and add others you need to make one long, correct sentence in English. Who can write the longest sentence? Who can write the funniest? Who can write the shortest?

A	H	O	M	E	B	S	G	W
S	T	E	A	K	U	H	E	H
V	N	T	B	I	R	D	T	A
W	I	H	U	S	G	W	S	T
I	C	A	N	F	L	O	O	R
N	E	T	C	H	A	T	C	G
D	O	G	H	M	R	H	K	O
O	O	T	H	E	L	E	S	O
W	M	A	K	E	F	R	B	D

1
25
2
20
3
20

THE FORTUNE TELLER AND THE BELLHOP

CAST OF CHARACTERS

MADAME ROSA, A FORTUNE TELLER
A BELLHOP
CHORUS

Bellhop Here comes Madame Rosa,
the famous fortune teller.
Her bags are full of crystal balls
and long silver earrings.

Chorus Crystal balls,
Crystal balls,
Long silver earrings.
Her bags are full of crystal balls
and long silver earrings.

Madame My bags are heavy,
much too heavy.
I can't carry my bags.

Chorus Her bags are heavy, much too heavy.
She can't carry her bags.

Bellhop I'll help you, Madame Rosa.
I'll help you with your bags.

Chorus He'll help you, Madame Rosa,
He'll help you with your bags.

Bellhop How many bags do you have, Madame?
How many bags do you have?

Madame Four bags,
I have four bags.
I have four big bags.

Chorus Four bags,
She has four bags,
She has four big bags.

Bellhop I'll help you, Madame Rosa,
with your four big bags.

Madame My bags are very heavy,
very, very heavy.
They're full of silver earrings
and large crystal balls.

Chorus Her bags are very heavy,
very, very heavy.
Long silver earrings,
Large crystal balls.

Madame Don't drop that suitcase!
It's full of crystal balls.
Be careful with my luggage.
It's full of crystal balls.

Chorus Be careful with her luggage.
It's full of crystal balls.
Don't drop her luggage.
It's full of crystal balls.

Bellhop There, I made it.
I didn't drop a thing.
I didn't break a crystal ball,
I didn't lose a ring.

Chorus He didn't lose an earring
or break a crystal ball.
He didn't drop her luggage,
or leave it in the hall.

Bellhop I did it, Madame Rosa.
Your bags are here, you see
I did my best for YOU.
I'm sure you'll do your best for ME.

Madame You did it, yes you did it.
My bags are here, it's true.
You did your best for me
and now I'll do my best for YOU.

Madame Give me your hand, young man.

Bellhop Of course, Madame Rosa.

Madame Let me see your other hand, young man.

Bellhop Of course, Madame Rosa.

Chorus Give her your hand, young man.
Let her see your hand.
Give her your other hand, young man.
Give her your other hand.

Madame You're going to have a wonderful life,
with fifteen kids and a beautiful wife.

Chorus You and your kids,
You and your wife
will live a long and happy life.

THE FORTUNE TELLER AND THE BELLHOP

Exercises

Ask Your Partner

A. Ask your partner the following questions and check the answers in the space provided.

	Yes	No
1. Did you go to a fortune teller last year?	☐	☐
2. Do you believe in fortune tellers?	☐	☐
3. Are there many fortune tellers in your country?	☐	☐
4. Do you know how to read a palm?	☐	☐
5. Do you know how to read tea leaves?	☐	☐
6. Are you a big tipper?	☐	☐
7. Are women big tippers in general?	☐	☐
8. Do people tip cab drivers in your country?	☐	☐

9. How much would you tip a bell hop when he helps you carry your bags?
10. Which two of the following qualities are important if you want to be:

	a. a good fortune teller	b. a good bellhop
a) youth	☐	☐
b) beauty	☐	☐
c) intelligence	☐	☐
d) imagination	☐	☐
e) strength	☐	☐

B. Write your own answers to questions 1-8 using a short response followed by a complete sentence.
Example: Did you ever have your palm read? Yes, I did. I had my palm read last year.

1. ______________________. ______________________.
2. ______________________. ______________________.
3. ______________________. ______________________.
4. ______________________. ______________________.
5. ______________________. ______________________.
6. ______________________. ______________________.
7. ______________________. ______________________.
8. ______________________. ______________________.

Pronunciation Practice

Five Famous Fortune Tellers

Five famous fortune tellers, sitting on the floor,
One went shopping,
Then there were four.

Four famous fortune tellers, flying home to France.
Five fat fortune-tellers, learning how to dance.

Four angry fortune tellers, fighting in the halls.
Four furious fortune tellers, breaking crystal balls.

Five hungry fortune tellers, eating pizza pie.
Five fearless fortune tellers, learning how to fly.

Word Puzzle

Use the clues to find the answers.

1. ______________
   a. I'm thinking of a word that starts with "s."
   b. It has 4 letters.
   c. It's usually on the water.
   d. It rhymes with trip.
2. ______________
   a. It starts with "i."
   b. It has 3 letters.
   c. It's very cold.
   d. It rhymes with nice.
3. ______________
   a. It starts with "l."
   b. It has 5 letters.
   c. It's the opposite of dark.
   d. It rhymes with right.
4. ______________
   a. It starts with "v."
   b. It has 3 letters.
   c. It's larger than a car.
   d. It rhymes with man.

5. ________________
   - a. It starts with "e."
   - b. It has 3 letters.
   - c. It's the opposite of begin.
   - d. It rhymes with send.

6. ________________
   - a. It starts with "r."
   - b. It has 4 letters.
   - c. It smells good.
   - d. Sometimes you buy a dozen.
   - e. It rhymes with nose.

Using your answers from the puzzle above, what word do their first letters spell? ________________________

Word Search

How many words can you find?

In the puzzle below, find words from the story and circle them. Some go across, others go down.

Work with a partner. How many other words can you find that are not in the story? List all the words you can find on a separate piece of paper, and add others you need to make one long, correct sentence in English. Who can write the longest sentence? Who can write the funniest? Who can write the shortest?

H	E	H	E	A	V	Y	F	A
A	T	C	A	R	E	F	U	L
N	S	O	R	E	R	O	L	U
D	I	D	R	M	Y	R	L	G
A	L	L	I	B	E	B	A	G
L	V	A	N	E	S	A	N	A
O	E	D	G	S	T	L	D	G
C	R	Y	S	T	A	L	I	E
B	Y	L	A	I	R	S	H	E

1
2
3
4

Unit Three

EVERYBODY IS HAVING A WONDERFUL TIME, EXCEPT ME

CAST OF CHARACTERS

KID
DADDY
CHORUS OF KIDS

Kid Everybody is having a wonderful time,
except me, Daddy.

Daddy WHAT?

Kid Everybody is having a wonderful time,
except me.

Chorus Everybody's having fun,
Everybody's having fun.

Kid Everybody's having a wonderful time,
except me.

Daddy What's the problem, what's wrong?

Chorus What's the problem? What's wrong?
What's the problem? What's wrong?

Kid Everybody has a bike.

Daddy Everybody has a what?

Kid A bike, a bike, everybody has a bike.
Everybody has a beautiful bike, except me.

Daddy I thought you had a bike.
I gave you a bike last year.

Chorus Last year, last year, he gave you a bike
last year.
He thought you had a bike.
He gave you a bike last year.

Kid I had a bike, but it broke, Daddy.

Chorus He had a bike, but it broke.
He had a bike, a beautiful bike.
He had a bike, but it broke.

Kid All the boys have bikes, Daddy.
All the girls have bikes.
I need a bike, Daddy, please.
I want a brand new bike.

Chorus He needs a bike, he wants a bike,
He wants a brand new bike.
All the kids have bikes, Daddy,
Buy him a brand new bike.

Daddy We'll see, we'll see.

Kid Every boy on the block has a bike,
Every girl has a bike.

Daddy We'll see, we'll see,
I'll talk to your mother,
We'll see.

Kid Nobody's riding a bike anymore.
Nobody's riding a bike.
Everybody's riding a skateboard now.
Nobody's riding a bike.

Chorus Nobody's riding a bike anymore.
Nobody's riding a bike.
Everybody's riding a skateboard now.
Nobody's riding a bike.

Kid None of the boys ride bikes anymore.
None of the boys like bikes.
None of the girls like bikes anymore.
None of the girls ride bikes.

Chorus None of the boys ride bikes anymore.
None of the boys like bikes.
None of the girls ride bikes anymore.
None of the girls like bikes.

Kid I hate this stupid bike.
None of the kids ride bikes.
I want to ride on a skateboard now,
I don't want to ride this bike.

Chorus He hates his stupid bike.
None of the kids ride bikes.
He wants to ride on a skateboard now,
He doesn't want to ride his bike.

Kid I wish I had a skateboard
instead of this stupid bike.
None of the kids ride bikes anymore.
I hate this stupid bike.

Kid Everybody's having a wonderful time,
except me, Daddy.

Daddy WHAT?

Kid Everybody's having a wonderful time,
except me.

Daddy What's the matter? What's wrong?

Kid Everybody has a skateboard now.
Everybody's riding a skateboard.
Buy me a skateboard, Daddy, please.
Everybody's having fun.

Daddy Now you want a skateboard?
I thought you wanted a bike.
You wanted a bike.
I bought you a bike.
You said you wanted a bike.

Chorus He said he wanted a bike.
He asked you for a bike.
He wanted a bike.
You bought him a bike.
He said he wanted a bike.

Kid Buy me a skateboard, Daddy, please.
I need a skateboard, Daddy.
I want to ride a skateboard, please.
I want to have some fun.

Chorus Buy him a skateboard, Daddy, please.
He needs a skateboard, Daddy.
He wants to ride a skateboard, please.
He wants to have some fun.

Kid At last I got my skateboard.
I finally have a skateboard.
My Daddy gave me a skateboard.
I'm finally going to have some fun!

Chorus At last he got his skateboard.
He finally has a skateboard.
His Daddy gave him a skateboard.
He's finally going to have some fun.

Kid Oh no, where did they go?
Where did all the skateboards go?

Chorus Oh no, oh no,
Where did all the skateboards go?

Kid Every kid is on roller skates.
Where did all the skateboards go?

Chorus Every kid is on roller skates.
Where did all the skateboards go?

Kid Everybody's having a wonderful time,
Everybody's having fun
Skating around on roller skates.
Everybody's having fun.

Chorus Skating around, skating around,
Everybody's having fun.
Skating around on roller skates,
Everybody's having fun.

Chorus Everybody's having a wonderful time.

Kid Except me, except me.

Chorus Everybody's having fun.

Kid Not me!

Chorus Everybody's having fun.

Kid Not me!

Chorus Everybody's having a wonderful time.

Kid Except me!

EVERYBODY IS HAVING A WONDERFUL TIME, EXCEPT ME

Exercises

Ask Your Partner

A. Ask your partner the following questions and check the answers in the space provided.

		Yes	No
1.	Do you know how to ride a bicycle?	☐	☐
2.	Do most people own a bicycle in your country?	☐	☐
3.	Do women ride bicycles in your country?	☐	☐
4.	Do you like to rollerskate?	☐	☐
5.	Do you own a pair of skates?	☐	☐
6.	When you were a child, did you usually get what you wanted?	☐	☐
7.	Did you have a happy childhood?	☐	☐
8.	Were you a spoiled child?	☐	☐
9.	Are bicycles expensive in your country?	☐	☐
10.	Do you think that a bicycle is as dangerous as a motorcycle?	☐	☐

B. Write your own answers to questions 1-10 using a short response followed by a complete sentence.
Example: Do you like to ride a bicycle? Yes, I do. I like to ride a bicycle.

1. ______________________. ______________________.
2. ______________________. ______________________.
3. ______________________. ______________________.
4. ______________________. ______________________.
5. ______________________. ______________________.
6. ______________________. ______________________.
7. ______________________. ______________________.
8. ______________________. ______________________.
9. ______________________. ______________________.
10. ______________________. ______________________.

Pronunciation Practice

A. Mike broke his bike.
B. What did he break?
A. Mike broke his bike
B. OH NO!

A. Larry broke his leg.
B. What did he break?
A. Larry broke his leg.
B. OH NO!

A. Anne broke her arm.
B. What did she break?
A. Anne broke her arm.
B. OH NO!

Mike broke his bike.
Anne broke her arm.
Larry broke his leg.
OH NO!

Word Puzzle

Use the clues to find the answers.

1. ______________
   a. It starts with an "h."
   b. It has 3 letters.
   c. Sometimes it's big. Sometimes it's small.
   d. It rhymes with fat.
2. ______________
   a. It starts with an "a."
   b. It has 4 letters.
   c. It rhymes with can't.
   d. It's your uncle's wife.
3. ______________
   a. It starts with a "p."
   b. It has 3 letters.
   c. It's usually sweet.
   d. It's a favorite American dessert.
   e. It rhymes with tie.
4. ______________
   a. It starts with a "p."
   b. It has 6 letters.
   c. Sometimes it's red, sometimes it's black.
   d. Sometimes it's very hot.
   e. You usually find it on the table.
5. ______________
   a. It starts with a "y."
   b. It has 4 letters.
   c. It has 365 days.
   d. It rhymes with fear.

Using your answers from the puzzle above, what word do their first letters spell?

____

Crossword Puzzle

Work with a partner. The words for this crossword puzzle are from Units One, Two and Three. Look at the clues below and fill in the blanks. For each clue, begin in the box with the same number.

Across

1. They keep your feet warm. Rhymes with box.
4. A preposition. Rhymes with do.
6. A group, several, many. Rhymes with lunch.
10. Be quiet! A little word a librarian says.
12. Something loud that bites.
13. Not bad. Rhymes with could.
14. Fast and fun footwear. Rhymes with late.

Down

2. Not two. Rhymes with fun.
3. Not smart. Rhymes with Cupid.
5. Not off. At the top. Rhymes with gone.
7. Belongs to him.
8. At this moment. Rhymes with cow.
9. It's good to eat. Rhymes with take.
11. It's nice for shaking. Rhymes with land.
14. Sometimes it hurts when it's new. Rhymes with blue.
15. After yesterday, before tomorrow. Rhymes with hooray.
16. Not any. Rhymes with run.
17. Sometimes it's hard to say. Rhymes with go.

1

2

3

BIG FISH, LITTLE FISH

CAST OF CHARACTERS

DADDY
DADDY'S LITTLE GIRL
FISH CHORUS

Girl HEY, I got a bite.

Daddy What did you say?

Girl I got a bite.
I think I caught a fish.

Chorus She thinks she caught a fish.
She got a bite.
She got a bite.
She thinks she caught a fish.

Daddy It's probably not a fish.
It's probably something else.

Chorus Not a fish,
Not a fish,
Probably something else.

Girl It feels like a fish, Daddy.
It feels like a great big fish.

Chorus It feels like a fish.
It feels like a fish.
It feels like a great big fish.

Girl Oh, no, it's not a fish.
It's just an old sock.

Chorus Not a fish, not a fish,
Just an old sock.
Old sock, old sock,
I wish you were a fish.

Girl Old sock, old sock,
I wish you were a fish.
I wish, I wish,
I wish you were,
I wish you were a fish.

Daddy That's alright, don't feel bad.
You'll get your fish,
You'll see.
Throw it back, try again,
You'll get your fish, you'll see.

Girl Daddy, hey, I got a bite.
I think I caught a fish.

Chorus DADDY, HEY, she got a bite,
She thinks she caught a fish.

Daddy It's probably not a fish.
It's probably something else.

Chorus Not a fish, not a fish,
Probably something else.

Girl OH no, it's a shoe.
I caught an old shoe.

Chorus OLD SHOE, she caught a shoe.
She caught an old shoe.

Girl Old shoe, old shoe,
I wish you were a fish.
I wish, I wish, I wish you were,
I wish you were a fish.

Daddy Throw it back, don't feel bad.
You'll get your fish, you'll see.

Girl Hey, Daddy, I got a bite.
I think I caught a fish.
Oh look! It IS a fish!
I caught a great big fish.

Daddy That fish is much too heavy for you,
Much too heavy to carry.

Girl It's not heavy. It's my FISH.

Daddy It's too heavy, much too heavy.
It's much too heavy to carry.

Girl No, it isn't.

Daddy Yes, it is.

Girl No, it isn't.

Daddy Yes, it is.
Give it to me.
I'll take the big one.
You take the small one.

Chorus He'll take the big one.
She'll take the small one.

Girl I don't want the small one.
I want the big one.

Daddy Here's a dollar.
I'll take the big one.

Girl I don't want a dollar.
YOU take the small one.

Daddy Here's two dollars.
You take the small one.

Girl I don't want two dollars.
You take the small one.

Daddy Here's five dollars.
You take the small one.

Girl OK DADDY, that's just fine.
I'll carry your fish,
You carry mine.

Chorus Big fish, little fish,
One, two, three,
She caught the biggest fish in the sea.

BIG FISH, LITTLE FISH
Exercises

Ask Your Partner

A. Ask your partner the following questions and check the answers in the space provided.

	Yes	No
1. Do you like fish?	☐	☐
2. Do you think fishing is a man's sport?	☐	☐
3. Have you ever caught a fish?	☐	☐
4. Do you like to eat raw fish?	☐	☐
5. Are you allergic to shellfish?	☐	☐

6. If you were a fish, would you prefer to be
   a. a pretty little goldfish ☐
   b. a great big tuna ☐
   c. a man-eating shark ☐

	Yes	No
7. Did you see *Jaws*?	☐	☐
8. Are you afraid of sharks?	☐	☐

9. Which of the following qualities does a good fisherman need the most?
   a. strength ☐
   b. intelligence ☐
   c. patience ☐
10. Would you rather be
   a. a big fish in a little pond ? ☐
   b. a little fish in a big pond? ☐

B. Write your own answers to questions 1-8 using a short response followed by a complete sentence. Example: Does your father like to fish? Yes, he does. My father likes to fish.

1. ______________________________. ______________________________.
2. ______________________________. ______________________________.
3. ______________________________. ______________________________.
4. ______________________________. ______________________________.
5. ______________________________. ______________________________.

6. ______________________________. ______________________________.
7. ______________________________. ______________________________.
8. ______________________________. ______________________________.

Pronunciation Practice

A. Is the fish fresh?

B. No, it's frozen.

A. Are the rolls fresh?

B. No, they're frozen.

A. Is the spinach fresh?

B. No, it's frozen.

A. Are the strawberries frozen?

B. No, they're fresh.

Try The Fish

Try the fish, I think it's delicious.
Don't pet the dog, he might be vicious.
Don't believe it. The story is malicious.
Knock on wood, I'm superstitious.

Are you allergic to shellfish?
Are you allergic to wheat?
Are you allergic to alcohol?
Are you allergic to meat?

My mother is allergic to shellfish.
My sister is allergic to wheat.
My father is allergic to alcohol.
And I'm allergic to meat.

Words And Expressions

That sounds *fishy* to me.	I don't believe it.
She's *fishing for a compliment.*	Hoping to receive a compliment.
He *fell for it hook, line and sinker.*	He believed the word completely.
She *hooked* him.	He asked her to marry him.
She's *hooked* on chocolate.	She can't give up chocolate.
What a good *catch!*	He or she is a good marriage partner.
He's not the only fish in the sea.	There are other men out there.

Word Search

How many words can you find?

In the puzzle below, find words from the story and circle them. Some go across, others go down.
Work with a partner. How many other words can you find that are not in the story? List all the words you can find on a separate piece of paper, and add others you need to make one long, correct sentence in English. Who can write the longest sentence? Who can write the funniest? Who can write the shortest?

R	S	M	A	L	L	G	O	T
S	O	M	E	T	H	I	N	G
O	C	A	U	G	H	T	B	F
T	K	U	M	U	C	H	I	I
D	O	L	L	A	R	N	G	S
P	R	O	B	A	B	L	Y	H
T	W	O	I	H	E	A	V	Y
L	I	T	T	L	E	O	N	E
E	L	S	E	F	I	V	E	N

1

2

3

4

SCARED OF THE DARK

CAST OF CHARACTERS

SCOUT LEADER
SCOUT ONE and SCOUT TWO
BEAR
CHORUS OF SCARED SCOUTS

Leader Deep in the forest,
away from home.
Isn't it fine?

Scout One I'm scared.

Scout Two Me, too.

Chorus We're scared,
away from home,
deep in the forest,
we're scared.

Leader Don't be silly.
You're safe in the forest.
There's no reason to be scared.

Scout One Mama said to be careful,
Mama said to watch out.

Chorus Watch out, watch out,
Mama said to watch out.
Mama said to be careful,
Mama said to watch out.

Leader Watch out?
For what?

Scout Two Snakes and bears.

Chorus Snakes and bears,
Mama said to watch out.

Scout Two Mama said to watch out for snakes,
Mama said to watch out.
Mama said to watch out for bears,
Mama said to watch out.

Leader There are no snakes or bears here.

Scout One NO? Are you sure?

Leader Of course I'm sure.
No snakes, no bears.

Chorus No snakes, no snakes,
no bears here.
No snakes, no snakes,
no bears here.

Leader Now, close your eyes and go to sleep.
Remember, NO bears.

Chorus Close your eyes and go to sleep,
No snakes, no snakes, no bears.

Leader Look at that,
They're sleeping.
The sweet little scouts are sleeping.

Chorus Sleeping, sleeping,
The sweet little scouts are sleeping.

Leader Look at that,
They're dreaming.
The sweet little scouts are dreaming.
Sweet dreams, sweet little scouts,
I'll see you in the morning.

Chorus Sweet dreams, sweet little scouts,
I'll see you in the morning.
Sweet dreams, sweet dreams,
I'll see you in the morning.

Leader Where's the moon?
Where are the stars?
It's very dark tonight.

Chorus Where's the moon?
Where are the stars?
It's dark, very dark.

Leader Oh, what's that over there?

Chorus What's that? What's that over there?

Leader Is that a man over there?

Chorus A man over there?

Bear I'm not a man, I'm a bear.
I'm the bear that wasn't there.

Leader What? A bear?

Bear I'm the bear that wasn't there.
You said there were no bears here.
Well, I'm the bear that wasn't there.

Chorus He's the bear.
He's the bear.
He's the bear that wasn't there.

Leader I'm scared.
I'm scared.
Deep in the forest,
I'm scared.

Bear Don't be silly,
You're safe with me.
There's no reason to be scared.

Leader You don't eat scouts?

Bear Who me? Eat scouts?
I don't eat meat,
I'm a vegetarian bear.

Chorus He never eats meat,
He never eats scouts,
He's a vegetarian bear.

Bear Go back to sleep,
Good night, sweet dreams.
I'll see you in the morning.

Chorus Close your eyes,
Go back to sleep.
He'll see you in the morning.
Sweet dreams,
go back to sleep.
He'll see you in the morning.

SCARED OF THE DARK

Exercises

Ask Your Partner

A. Ask your partner the following questions and check the answers in the space provided.

	Yes	No
1. When you were a child, were you scared of the dark?	☐	☐
2. Do you enjoy camping?	☐	☐
3. Do you like to sleep in a sleeping bag?	☐	☐
4. Have you ever slept in a tent in the woods?	☐	☐
5. Do you like to cook outdoors?	☐	☐
6. Are you afraid of spiders?	☐	☐
7. Are you an "outdoor type"?	☐	☐

8. Which do you prefer, a simple tent in the woods or a comfortable room in a big hotel?
9. What's the most famous mountain in your country?
10. Which is more dangerous, mountain climbing or Scuba diving?

B. Write your own answers to questions 1-7 using a short response followed by a complete sentence.
Example: Have you ever gone mountain climbing? Yes, I have. I went mountain climbing last year.

1. ______________________. ______________________.
2. ______________________. ______________________.
3. ______________________. ______________________.
4. ______________________. ______________________.
5. ______________________. ______________________.
6. ______________________. ______________________.
7. ______________________. ______________________.

Word Puzzle

Use the clues find the answers.

1. ______________
   a. It starts with an "s."
   b. It has 5 letters.
   c. It is the opposite of sour.
   d. Children love it.
2. ______________
   a. It starts with a "c."
   b. It has 5 letters.
   c. It is very sweet.
   d. Children love it.
3. ______________
   a. It starts with an "a."
   b. It has 5 letters.
   c. Sometimes it is red.
   d. It is delicious to eat.
4. ______________
   a. It starts with an "r."
   b. It has 5 letters.
   c. It rhymes with light.
   d. It is the opposite of wrong.
5. ______________
   a. It starts with an "e."
   b. It has 3 letters.
   c. It rhymes with send.
   d. It's the opposite of begin.
6. ______________
   a. It starts with a "d."
   b. It has 4 letters.
   c. It rhymes with park.
   d. It's the opposite of light.

Using your answers from the puzzle above, what word do their first letters spell? ____________________

Words And Expressions

Scared to death Scared silly Scared stiff Scared out of my wits Scared speechless Frightened to death Frozen with fear	Very frightened
He's scared of his own shadow.	He's afraid of everything.
Scared of heights	
Scared of the dark	

Word Search

How many words can you find?

In the puzzle below, find words from the story and circle them. Some go across, others go down.
Work with a partner. How many other words can you find that are not in the story? List all the words you can find on a separate piece of paper, and add others you need to make one long, correct sentence in English. Who can write the longest sentence? Who can write the funniest? Who can write the shortest?

L	I	N	O	V	E	R	S	O
A	N	O	S	N	A	K	E	S
S	I	L	L	Y	T	B	E	C
D	R	U	E	W	S	O	F	O
R	O	B	E	A	R	S	O	U
E	M	A	P	T	S	U	R	T
A	E	F	S	C	A	R	E	D
M	A	M	A	H	F	E	S	O
S	T	H	E	R	E	I	T	O

1
NEW MEXICO
2
3
4
5

THE RAIN DANCE

CAST OF CHARACTERS

CHILD
DADDY and MOMMY
INDIAN CHIEF
CHORUS OF TOURISTS

Child Are we there yet, Daddy?

Daddy No, not yet.

Chorus Are we there?
Are we there?
Are we there yet, Daddy?

Daddy No, not yet, not yet, not yet.

Child Are those Indians, Daddy?

Daddy No, they aren't.
I told you we're not there yet.

Child How much longer 'till we get there, Daddy?

Chorus How much longer?
How much longer?

Daddy Don't worry, we're almost there.

Child I'm getting awfully hungry, Mommy.

Mommy Don't worry, we're almost there.

Child I think I'm getting carsick, Daddy.

Daddy Don't worry, we're almost there.

Child I'm getting awfully thirsty, Mommy.

Mommy Don't worry, we're almost there.

Child I have to go to the bathroom, Daddy.

Daddy Don't worry, we're almost there.

Chorus Almost there, almost there,
Don't worry, we're almost there.

Child Look, Daddy, Indians!
We're here at last, we're here.
A real Indian village!
We're here, at last we're here.

Chorus We're here, we're here,
I can't believe we're here.
A real Indian village,
We're here, at last we're here.

Child Is that an Indian?

Mommy Where?

Child There. The man in the blanket
with the long black hair.

Mommy Are those Indians?

Daddy Where?

Mommy There. The men in the blankets
with the long black hair.

Daddy Those are Indians. Those are Indians there.

Indian Chief Welcome to our village.

Child Mommy! He speaks English!

Daddy Sh! Don't be rude.
We're very happy to be here.

Mommy What a lovely place!

Daddy And what a lovely day!
Not a cloud in the sky.

Child Are you really an Indian?

Indian Chief Yes, I am.

Child Are those real feathers?

Indian Chief Yes, they are.

Child Is that your real hair?

Indian Chief Yes, it is.

Daddy Sh! Stop asking so many questions.

Child Mommy! Daddy! Look at all the Indians!
Here they come. They're everywhere.

Chorus Indians, Indians, everywhere,
Indians everywhere.

Mommy I hope they're going to dance.
I'd love to see them dance.

Chorus Indians, Indians, everywhere,
I hope they're going to dance.

Mommy Look, look they're dancing.
They're dancing, they're dancing.
Look, look they're dancing.
What kind of a dance is that?

Indian Chief It's a Rain Dance.

Mommy A what?

Indian Chief A Rain Dance,
A Rain Dance.

Mommy Look, they're doing a Rain Dance.

Daddy I hope it doesn't rain, Ha Ha.

Mommy Why do they call it a Rain Dance?

Indian Chief Wait for a moment, you'll see.

Mommy What's that?

Daddy Rain.

Mommy Did you say rain?
Is it starting to rain?

Child Starting to rain? Oh, no!

Chorus It's starting to rain, oh, no!
It's raining, it's raining.
The dancers are doing a Rain Dance,
and it's starting to rain. Oh, NO!

Child It's pouring, Oh, NO!
Tell them to stop that Rain Dance.
Stop the Rain Dance right now.
I'm getting wet.
I'm getting wet.
Stop the Rain Dance right now.
My feet are getting wet.

Chorus Our hair is getting wet.
Our feet are getting wet.
Stop the Rain Dance right now.
Our feet are getting wet.

Daddy Let's get out of the rain.
Come on, let's go!
Let's get inside,
Let's go!

Chorus Come on, let's go!
Let's get out of the rain,
Let's get out of the rain,
Let's go!

Mommy I'm getting wet.
Let's get out of the rain.

Daddy Let's get inside,
Let's go!

Indian Chief (TO THE DANCERS) Good work, boys.
I'll pay you later.
Terrific job. Well done.

Indian Chief Today's your lucky day.

Daddy It is?

Indian Chief Of course it is.
You're lucky today.

Daddy We are?

Indian Chief You're just in time.

Mommy In time for what?

Indian Chief For our annual umbrella sale.

Daddy Your umbrella sale?

Indian Chief Our umbrella sale,
Our giant annual umbrella sale.
People come from miles around
for our annual umbrella sale.

Mommy They do?

Indian Chief Of course they do.
All the umbrellas are half price.
Take two, they're small.
And beautiful.

Chorus Take two, they're small.
Take two, they're small.

Indian Chief For a day like today, they're perfect.
For a day like today, they're fine.

Chorus For a day like today, a day like today,
For a day like today, they're fine.

Child The sun was shining a minute ago,
and now it's raining hard.

Chorus The sun was shining a minute ago,
and now it's raining hard.
Raining hard, raining hard,
Now it's raining hard.

Child Look, Mommy, look at those men,
those men selling umbrellas.

Mommy The men in the suits?
The men in the ties?
The men in the suits and ties?

Chorus Suits and ties, suits and ties,
Selling umbrellas in suits and ties.
Men wearing suits,
Men wearing ties,
Men wearing suits and ties.

Child Look, Daddy, they're the same men.

Daddy What do you mean they're the same
men?

Child The men in the suits and ties.
They're the men
who were dancing the Rain Dance
just a minute ago.

Chorus Just a minute ago,
Just a minute ago,
They're the men
who were dancing the Rain Dance
Just a minute ago.

Daddy Good heavens, I think you're right.
You're a smart little kid.

Child I know, but some folks are smarter
than I am.

Mommy You mean your Mommy and Daddy?

Child No, I mean the Indians!

THE RAIN DANCE

Exercises

Ask Your Partner

A. Ask your partner the following questions and check the answers in the space provided.

		Yes	No
1.	Do you like to travel by bus?	☐	☐
2.	Is bus travel inexpensive in your country?	☐	☐
3.	In your country do the buses usually run on time?	☐	☐
4.	Do you have a long rainy season in your country?	☐	☐
5.	Do you like to walk in the rain?	☐	☐
6.	Do you think a bus is more comfortable than a train?	☐	☐
7.	Have you ever seen American Indian jewelry?	☐	☐
8.	Have you ever watched an American Indian rain dance?	☐	☐
9.	Have you ever met an American Indian?	☐	☐
10.	How much does an umbrella cost in your country?		

B. Write your own answers to questions 1-9 using a short response followed by a complete sentence.
Example: Do you like the rain? Yes, I do. I like the rain.

1. ______________________. ______________________.
2. ______________________. ______________________.
3. ______________________. ______________________.
4. ______________________. ______________________.
5. ______________________. ______________________.
6. ______________________. ______________________.
7. ______________________. ______________________.
8. ______________________. ______________________.
9. ______________________. ______________________.

Word Puzzle

Use the clues to find the answers.

1. ______________
   a. It starts with a "d."
   b. It has 4 letters.
   c. It's the opposite of up.
2. ______________
   a. It starts with an "a."
   b. It has 6 letters.
   c. It's the opposite of never.
3. ______________
   a. It starts with "n."
   b. It has 4 letters.
   c. It rhymes with rice.
4. ______________
   a. It starts with "c."
   b. It has 5 letters.
   c. It's the opposite of dirty.
5. ______________
   a. It starts with "e."
   b. It has 5 letters.
   c. It's the opposite of full.

Using your answers from the puzzle above, what word do their first letters spell? ______________

Words And Expressions

It never rains but it pours.	Trouble follows trouble.
Save your money for a rainy day.	Keep some of your money for emergencies.
Don't rain on my parade.	Don't spoil my fun.
April showers bring May flowers.	
Sunshine follows the rain.	Something good will come from something bad.
Nice weather for ducks.	A sarcastic expression used when it's raining hard.
He doesn't know enough to come in out of the rain.	He's stupid.
It's raining, it's pouring, The old man is snoring.	A child's rhyme about the rain and the sound of thunder.

Crossword Puzzle

Work with a partner. The words for this crossword puzzle are from Units Four, Five, and Six. Look at the clues below and fill in the blanks. For each clue, begin in the box with the same number.

Across

1. Opposite of nothing.
3. When you forget it, you get wet.
4. Opposite of dry. Rhymes with get.
5. Moving to music.
6. The taste of candy. Opposite of sour.
8. How you feel before an examination or after a terrible dream.

Down

2. Very big; very large size.
5. Sometimes they're sweet, sometimes they're scary.
7. Opposite of new. Rhymes with cold.

	1								2
		3							
	4								
5									
		6							7
				8					

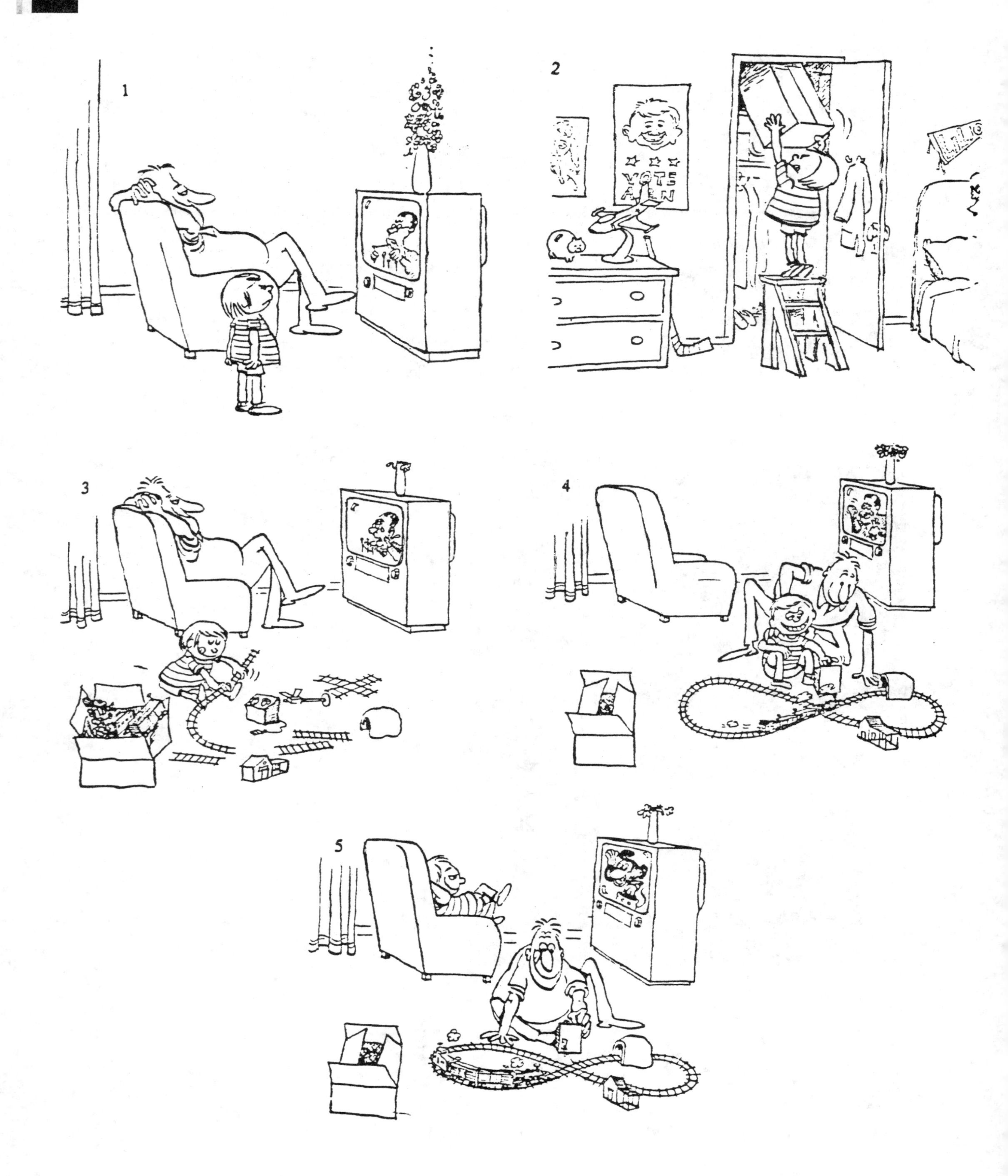
1
2
VOTE
3
4
5

TOYS

CAST OF CHARACTERS

DAD
CHILD
TV REPORTER
CHORUS

Child Daddy, can I watch Mickey Mouse?

Daddy SH! I'm watching the news.

Chorus Watching the news, watching the news,
Daddy says he's watching the news.

Child It's almost time for Mickey Mouse.

Chorus It's almost time, almost time,
It's almost time for Mickey Mouse.

Daddy I said I'm watching the news.

Child Mickey Mouse starts at six o'clock.

Chorus Six o'clock, six o'clock,
Mickey Mouse starts at six o'clock.

Daddy Daddy is watching the news.
Why don't you play with your toys?

Chorus Why don't you play with your toys?
Why don't you play with your toys?
Play with your toys,
Play with your toys,
Why don't you play with your toys?

Child I don't want to play with my toys, no.
I just want to watch TV.

Chorus He doesn't want to play with his toys, no.
He just wants to watch TV.
He wants to watch,
He wants to watch,
He wants to watch TV.

Daddy If you really want to watch TV,
You can watch the news with me.
You can watch the news with Daddy,
You can watch TV with me.

Chorus You can watch the news with Daddy
If you really want to watch TV.
Watch the news with Daddy
If you really want to watch TV.

Child I don't want to watch the news, Daddy,
I don't want to watch the news.
I want to watch TV, Daddy,
but I don't want to watch the news.

Chorus He doesn't want to watch the news, Daddy,
He doesn't want to watch the news.
He wants to watch TV, Daddy,
but he doesn't want to watch the news.

Daddy Then play with your toys
but don't bother Daddy.
Daddy wants to watch the news.

Chorus Play with your toys,
but don't bother Daddy.
Daddy wants to watch the news.

TV Reporter And now for the news, the six o'clock news.
It's raining in Japan.

Child Raining in Japan? Who cares if it's raining in Japan?

Daddy SH! Be quiet. Please be quiet,
Daddy's watching the news.

Chorus It's raining in Japan, raining in Japan.
Daddy's watching the news.

TV Reporter It's finally stopped raining in Osaka.
The sun is shining in L.A.

Child Who cares if it's raining in Osaka?
I hate the six o'clock news.

Daddy SH! Be quiet. Play with your toys.

TV Reporter And now for a word from our sponsor...

Child I'm going to miss Mickey Mouse, oh no!

Chorus He's going to miss Mickey Mouse, oh no!

Child (Talking to himself) I have an idea,
I think it'll work.
Sure, I'll play with my toys.

Chorus He has an idea,
He thinks it'll work.
Sure, he'll play with his toys.

Child I'll set up my new train set.
I'll be as sweet as I can be.
Daddy loves my train set.
He won't want to watch TV.

Chorus He'll set up his new train set.
He'll be sweet as he can be.
Daddy loves his train set.
He won't want to watch TV.

Daddy Isn't that the train set I got for you last year?

Chorus Train set, train set,
Isn't that the train set?
Isn't that the train set
He got for you last year?

Child Am I bothering you, Daddy?
I know you're watching the news.

Daddy I love to watch a train arrive
on a little railroad track.
I love to see it go away
then watch it coming back.

Chorus He loves to watch the train arrive
on the little railroad track.
He loves to see it go away
then watch it coming back.

Child Here we are, my Dad and me,
happy as can be.
He loves to watch the little train.
I love to watch TV.

Chorus There they are,
the two of them,
happy as can be.
His Daddy loves to play with trains.
He loves to watch TV.

TOYS
Exercises

Ask Your Partner

A. Ask your partner the following questions and check the answers in the space provided.

	Question	Yes	No
1.	Did you ever have a toy train?	☐	☐
2.	When you were a child, did you watch Mickey Mouse on TV?	☐	☐
3.	Do you think children have more fun than adults?	☐	☐
4.	Do you watch the news on TV?	☐	☐
5.	Do children play with toy guns in your country?	☐	☐
6.	Did your mother tell you bedtime stories when you were growing up?	☐	☐
7.	Do you enjoy walking through a toy store?	☐	☐
8.	Would you like to work in a toy department?	☐	☐
9.	Do you think children spend too much time watching TV?	☐	☐
10.	What was your favorite toy when you were growing up?		

B. Write your own answers to questions 1-9 using a short response followed by a complete sentence.
Example: Did you like playing with toys when you were a child? Yes, I did. I liked playing with toys.

1. ______________________. ______________________.
2. ______________________. ______________________.
3. ______________________. ______________________.
4. ______________________. ______________________.
5. ______________________. ______________________.
6. ______________________. ______________________.
7. ______________________. ______________________.
8. ______________________. ______________________.
9. ______________________. ______________________.

Pronunciation Practice

Mama's in the kitchen
shining Papa's shoes,
washing Papa's dishes
while he watches the news.

Papa's in the kitchen
shining Mama's shoes,
washing Mama's dishes
while she watches the news.

There's a light rain falling,
Listen to the rain.
Listen to the whistle
of the six o'clock train.

Look at the clock.
It's already eight.
The six o'clock train
is two hours late.

Word Puzzle

Use the clues to find the answers.

1. ______________
   a. It starts with "t."
   b. It has 3 letters.
   c. It rhymes with boy.
2. ______________
   a. It starts with "r."
   b. It has 4 letters.
   c. It rhymes with pain.
3. ______________
   a. It starts with "a."
   b. It has 3 letters.
   c. It's the opposite of answer.
4. ______________
   a. It starts with "i."
   b. It has 4 letters.
   c. It's the opposite of "out of."
5. ______________
   a. It starts with "n."
   b. It has 4 letters.
   c. It's the opposite of far.

Using your answers from the puzzle above, what word do their first letters spell?______________________

Word Search

How many words can you find?

In the puzzle below, find words from the story and circle them. Some go across, others go down.
Work with a partner. How many other words can you find that are not in the story? List all the words you can find on a separate piece of paper, and add others you need to make one long, correct sentence in English. Who can write the longest sentence? Who can write the funniest? Who can write the shortest?

N	W	A	T	C	H	I	N	G
E	I	N	V	T	R	A	I	N
W	D	A	R	R	I	V	E	L
S	E	E	H	A	P	P	Y	I
H	A	V	E	C	R	N	C	T
D	B	A	C	K	P	S	E	T
R	A	I	L	R	O	A	D	L
I	O	S	W	S	E	T	V	E
P	L	A	Y	T	O	Y	S	R

LIES

CAST OF CHARACTERS

A KIND WOMAN
A LITTLE BOY
GROUP LEADER
CHORUS OF KIDS

Boy BOO HOO! BOO HOO!

Woman It sounds like somebody is crying.

Boy BOO HOO! BOO HOO!

Woman Somebody's crying.
It sounds like a little boy crying.

Chorus Somebody's crying.
Somebody's crying.
It sounds like a little boy crying.

Woman Who's crying? Where are you?

Boy Here I am, it's me.

Woman Why are you sitting on the street like that?
Why are you crying, little boy?

Chorus Why are you crying?
Why are you crying?
Why are you crying little boy?

Boy I'm crying because I'm sad.

Woman Please stop crying
and tell me, tell me,
What's the matter? What's wrong?

Boy I can't stop crying.
I'm so sad.

Woman Please stop crying.

Boy I can't.

Woman Tell me, please,
What's the matter?
Please stop crying.

Boy I lost it all.

Woman What do you mean?

Boy I lost it all.

Woman What did you lose?

Boy The money.

Woman The money?

Boy I lost all the money.

Woman What money?

Boy The money Mama gave me for the medicine.

Woman The medicine? What medicine?

Boy The medicine for the baby.

Woman The baby? What baby?

Boy Mama's little baby.
My baby brother.

Woman Is he very sick?

Boy He's sick as a dog.
The dog's sick too.

Woman You have a dog?
What kind of a dog?

Boy A sick dog,
a very sick dog.
Mama's sick,
The baby is sick,
and I'm not feeling very well myself.

Woman Oh dear, oh dear.
I'm starting to cry.

Boy Please don't cry.
We'll be all right.

Woman Take this money.

Boy Oh no, I couldn't.

Woman OH, please,
Take it all.

Boy GEE THANKS.

Boy I've got money,
I'm ready to play.

Leader Where did you get that money?

Boy Never mind.

Leader Why did you tell those lies?

Boy What lies?

Leader You know what I mean.
We heard it all.
You don't have a brother.
Your dog isn't sick.
We don't want your money.
We don't want your lies.

Chorus Lies, lies,
Why did you tell?
Why did you tell those lies?
You don't have a brother.
Your dog isn't sick.
We don't want your money or your lies.

LIES
Exercises

Ask Your Partner

A. Ask your partner the following questions and check the answers in the space provided.

	Yes	No
1. Did you ever lose your wallet?	☐	☐
2. Do you ever give money to poor people on the street?	☐	☐
3. Do you like to gamble?	☐	☐
4. Have you ever won money in a card game?	☐	☐
5. Do you like to play poker?	☐	☐
6. Have you ever played Bingo?	☐	☐
7. Do many people like to gamble in your country?	☐	☐
8. Can you usually tell when a person is lying?	☐	☐
9. Is it easy to tell a lie?	☐	☐
10. Do you always tell the truth?	☐	☐

B. Write your own answers to questions 1-10 using a short response followed by a complete sentence.
Example: Do you like to play cards? No, I don't. I don't like to play cards.

1. ______________________. ______________________.
2. ______________________. ______________________.
3. ______________________. ______________________.
4. ______________________. ______________________.
5. ______________________. ______________________.
6. ______________________. ______________________.
7. ______________________. ______________________.
8. ______________________. ______________________.
9. ______________________. ______________________.
10. ______________________. ______________________.

Word Puzzle

Use the clues to find the answers.

1. ______________
   a. It starts with "s."
   b. It has 4 letters.
   c. It rhymes with cave.
2. ______________
   a. It starts with "i."
   b. It has 4 letters.
   c. It rhymes with pinch.
3. ______________
   a. It starts with "c."
   b. It has 3 letters.
   c. It rhymes with far.
4. ______________
   a. It starts with"k."
   b. It has 4 letters.
   c. It rhymes with find.

Using your answers from the puzzle above, what word do their first letters spell?______________________

Words And Expressions

He's lying through his teeth.	He's not telling the truth.
Little white lie	A small lie
Lucky in cards, unlucky in love.	A popular saying about luck
Sometimes the truth hurts.	
Tell me the truth, even if it hurts.	

Word Search

How many words can you find?

In the puzzle below, find words from the story and circle them. Some go across, others go down.
Work with a partner. How many other words can you find that are not in the story? List all the words you can find on a separate piece of paper, and add others you need to make one long, correct sentence in English. Who can write the longest sentence? Who can write the funniest? Who can write the shortest?

T	C	R	Y	I	N	G	I	H
H	M	E	D	I	C	I	N	E
E	C	A	L	L	O	V	A	L
R	O	D	M	O	N	E	Y	D
E	W	S	A	S	I	C	K	W
W	H	A	T	E	N	T	S	A
H	Y	D	T	E	N	D	O	N
O	L	I	E	S	L	O	S	T
T	O	W	R	O	N	G	O	T

1
2
3
4
5

MADAME ROSA AND THE CALIFORNIA BEAR

CAST OF CHARACTERS

MADAME ROSA, A FORTUNE TELLER
A MAN
CHORUS

Man Why are you looking at me like that?
What's the matter?
What do you see?

Chorus What's the matter?
What do you see?
Why are you looking like that?

Madame Rosa Terrible, it looks terrible.

Man What do you mean, "it looks terrible"?

Madame Rosa Awful, it looks awful.

Man What do you mean, "it looks awful"?

Madame Rosa Your future, your life. It looks terrible.

Man WHY? WHY?
What do you see?

Madame Rosa I see a ...

Man What? What? What do you see?

Madame Rosa I see a great big ...

Man What? What? Tell me please.

Madame Rosa Terrible, it looks terrible.

Chorus Terrible, it looks terrible.

Man Madame Rosa, answer me.
Madame Rosa, what do you see?

Chorus Answer me, answer me.
Madame Rosa, what do you see?

Madame Rosa I see a bear, a great big bear,
a California grizzly bear.

Chorus She sees a California bear,
a great big California bear.

Man A California bear? Where?

Madame Rosa Here.

Man That's impossible. We're not in California.

Madame Rosa A great big California bear.

Man Ridiculous.

Madame Rosa A hungry bear.

Man Impossible.

Madame Rosa I swear it's a bear.

Man Ridiculous.
Impossible.
A bear in this city? Oh no!

Madame Rosa Listen to me, carefully.
You're going to be attacked by a bear.

Man Who me?
Attacked by a bear?
Give me a break! Don't be silly!

Madame Rosa Listen to me, carefully.

You're going to be attacked by a bear, I swear.
You're going to be attacked by a bear.

Chorus Attacked by a bear,
Attacked by a bear,
He's going to be attacked by a bear.

Man Here, in the city?
Attacked by a bear?
Give me a break!

Madame Rosa You'll see, you'll see.
Listen to me,
carefully.
You're going to be attacked by a bear.

Man WHEN?

Madame Rosa Tonight.

Man Tonight?

Madame Rosa That's right,
That's right.

Man I don't believe a word you've said.

Chorus Not a word, not a word,
He doesn't believe a word you've said.

Man Madame Rosa, you're crazy!
Madame Rosa, you're nuts!
Off the wall!
Out to lunch!
Madame Rosa, you're nuts!

Chorus Madame Rosa, you're crazy!
Madame Rosa, you're nuts!
Off the wall, out to lunch,
Madame Rosa, you're nuts!

Man I don't believe a word you've said.

Chorus Not a word, not a word you've said.

Man I don't believe a word you've said.
What's that over there?
What's that?

Chorus What's that over there?
What's that?

Man Something's moving,
Something's there.
Something's there in the dark.

Chorus Something's moving,
Something's there,
Something's there in the dark.

Man Something's moving
there in the dark,
Something big in the dark.

Chorus Something's moving,
Something big,
Something's there in the dark.

Man Something's coming this way,
Hey!
Something's coming this way.

Chorus Something's coming,
Something's coming,
Something's coming this way.

Man What's that over there?
It looks like a bear.
It IS a bear!
Madame Rosa was right!

Chorus He's ready to fight,
Ready to fight,
Madame Rosa was right!

Madame Rosa Now he knows
that bears can fight,
and Madame Rosa is always right.

MADAME ROSA AND THE CALIFORNIA BEAR

Exercises

Ask Your Partner

A. Ask your partner the following questions and check the answers in the space provided.

	Yes	No
1. Are bears stronger than men?	☐	☐
2. Is a bear more intelligent than a man?	☐	☐
3. Are California bears dangerous?	☐	☐
4. Have you ever seen a Polar Bear?	☐	☐
5. Have you ever seen a dancing bear?	☐	☐
6. Do people hunt bear in your country?	☐	☐
7. Have you ever walked on a bear rug?	☐	☐
8. Would you shoot a bear for pleasure?	☐	☐
9. Do you like to go to the zoo?	☐	☐
10. Would you like to work in a zoo?	☐	☐

B. Write your own answers to questions 1-10 using a short response followed by a complete sentence.
Example: Have you ever seen a bear at the zoo? Yes, I have. I saw a bear at the zoo.

1. ______________________. ______________________.
2. ______________________. ______________________.
3. ______________________. ______________________.
4. ______________________. ______________________.
5. ______________________. ______________________.
6. ______________________. ______________________.
7. ______________________. ______________________.
8. ______________________. ______________________.
9. ______________________. ______________________.
10. ______________________. ______________________.

Pronunciation Practice

What did you see?
I saw a bear.

What did you say?
I said a prayer.

What did he want?
He wanted to play.

What did you do?
I ran away.

The bear was big.
The bear was strong.
The bear was very scary.

The bear was tough.
The bear was rough.
The bear was very hairy.

Word Puzzle

Use the clues to find the answers.

1. ______________
   a. It starts with "d."
   b. It has 4 letters.
   c. It rhymes with for.
2. ______________
   a. It starts with "a."
   b. It has 3 letters.
   c. It rhymes with page.
3. ______________
   a. It starts with "r."
   b. It has 3 letters.
   c. It rhymes with bed.
4. ______________
   a. It starts with "k."
   b. It has 4 letters.
   c. It rhymes with sleep.

Using your answers from the puzzle above, what word do their first letters spell? ______________________

Word Search

How many words can you find?

In the puzzle below, find words from the story and circle them. Some go across, others go down.
Work with a partner. How many other words can you find that are not in the story? List all the words you can find on a separate piece of paper, and add others you need to make one long, correct sentence in English. Who can write the longest sentence? Who can write the funniest? Who can write the shortest?

N	O	F	U	T	U	R	E	X
W	C	O	M	I	N	G	S	B
H	L	R	I	G	H	T	L	I
A	T	T	A	C	K	B	I	G
T	R	U	W	O	W	E	F	R
L	B	N	A	U	H	A	E	E
X	O	E	L	G	E	R	P	A
T	E	L	L	E	R	F	N	T
L	U	N	C	H	E	R	E	F

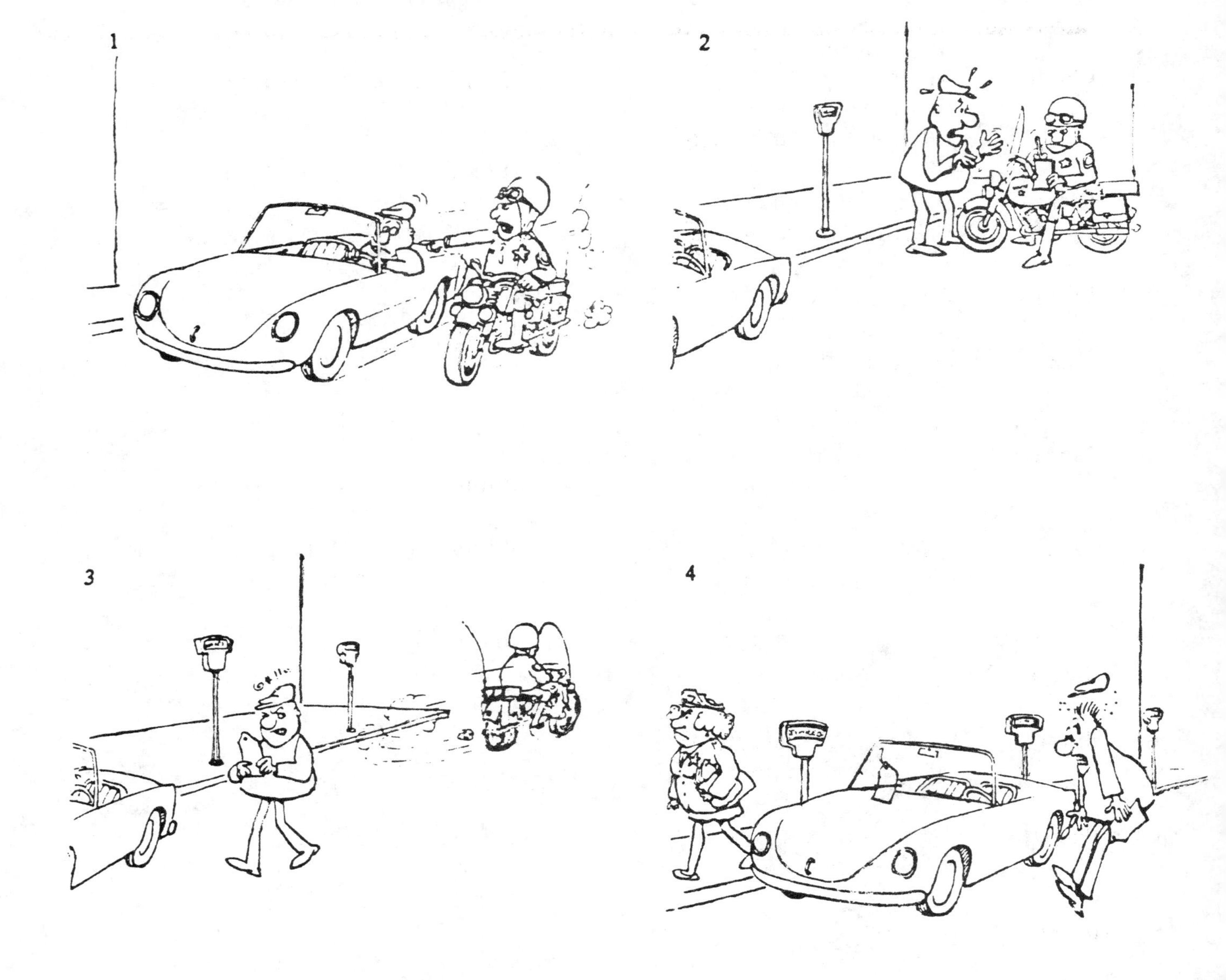
1
2
3
4

THE TRAFFIC TICKET

CAST OF CHARACTERS

POLICE OFFICER
METER MAID
DRIVER
CHORUS OF PEDESTRIANS

Officer O.K. Mister,
Slow down,
Please pull over to the curb.

Chorus Slow down, slow down,
Please pull over to the curb.

Driver What did you say?

Officer You heard me.
Please pull over to the curb.

Chorus You heard him, you heard him.
Please pull over to the curb.

Driver What's the matter? What's wrong?
I wasn't doing anything.

Officer May I see your driver's license?

Driver Of course, but what's the matter?
Officer! What are you doing?

Officer What do you think I'm doing?
I'm giving you a ticket.

Driver A ticket? For what?

Officer For speeding.
You were speeding.
You were driving too fast.
You were speeding.

Chorus Too fast, much too fast,
Too fast, you were speeding.

Driver Officer, you're mistaken.
I'm sure I wasn't speeding.

Officer I saw you.
You were going too fast.
I was following you.
You were speeding.

Chorus He saw you.
You were going too fast.
He saw you.
You were speeding.

Driver Officer, you're mistaken.

Officer You were going too fast.
You were speeding.

Driver No, I wasn't.

Officer Yes, you were.

Driver No, I wasn't.

Officer Yes, you were.

Driver I was not.

Officer You were too.
Don't argue with me,
I was following you.

Driver I'm not arguing with you.

Officer Yes, you are.

Driver No, I'm not.

Officer Yes, you are.
You were driving too fast,
and that's that.
Here's your ticket.
Have a nice day!

Driver Hey, what are you doing?

Meter Maid I'm writing you a ticket.

Driver A ticket?
What for?

Meter Maid Illegal parking.

Driver Illegal parking?
What do you mean?

Meter Maid You forgot to put money in the meter.

Chorus Money in the meter,
Money in the meter,
You forgot to put money in the meter.

Driver Money in the meter? Oh, no!
I forgot to put money in the meter!
Two tickets, one day,
Two tickets in a day!

Chorus Two tickets, one day,
Two tickets in a day.
Speeding and parking,
Speeding and parking,
Two tickets in a day!

Driver Today is not my day, oh,
I should have used my head.
Today is not my day, no,
I should have stayed in bed.

THE TRAFFIC TICKET
Exercises

Ask Your Partner

A. Ask your partner the following questions and check the answers in the space provided.

	Yes	No
1. Can you drive a car?	☐	☐
2. Do you have a driver's license?	☐	☐
3. Have you ever gotten a traffic ticket?	☐	☐
4. Do people drive very fast in your country?	☐	☐
5. Are women better drivers than men?	☐	☐
6. Have you ever had an accident?	☐	☐

7. Which of the following qualities do you look for in a car? List in order of importance.
   beauty, speed, style, safety, economy, comfort
8. How old do you have to be to get a driver's license in your country?
9. What would be your ideal car (color, style, make)?
10. How much does a car cost in your country?

B. Write your own answers to questions 1-6 using a short response followed by a complete sentence.
Example: Do you like like to drive a car? Yes, I do. I like to drive a car.

1. ______________________. ______________________.
2. ______________________. ______________________.
3. ______________________. ______________________.
4. ______________________. ______________________.
5. ______________________. ______________________.
6. ______________________. ______________________.

Pronunciation Practice

Practice the sound of "r."
One ticket, two tickets
Both in one day.
Tom tore the tickets up
and threw them both away.

You're going to get a traffic ticket.
    How do you know?

You're driving in the fast lane
going very slow.
Go on ahead, the light's not red.
    What do you mean?

The light is green.

Word Puzzle

Use the clues to find the answers.

1. ______________
   a. It starts with "s."
   b. It has 4 letters.
   c. It's the opposite of fast.
2. ______________
   a. It starts with "p."
   b. It has 4 letters.
   c. It rhymes with dark.
3. ______________
   a. It starts with "e."
   b. It has 4 letters.
   c. It's the opposite of hard.
4. ______________
   a. It starts with "e."
   b. It has 3 letters.
   c. It's the opposite of beginning.
5. ______________
   a. It starts with "d."
   b. It has 5 letters.
   c. It rhymes with five.

Using your answers from the puzzle above, what word do their first letters spell? ____________________

Crossword Puzzle

Work with a partner. The words for this crossword puzzle are from Units Seven, Eight, Nine and Ten. Look at the clues below and fill in the blanks. For each clue, begin in the box with the same number.

Across

1. (2 words, 9 letters.) She writes parking tickets.
4. What we read in the papers.
5. A thought. You feel smart when you get one.
8. Disagree.
9. Recent. Rhymes with true.
11. Big town. Rhymes with kitty.
12. Not well.
14. Negative. Rhymes with go.
15. You see one in the zoo. Rhymes with scare.

Down

1. We wouldn't be here without her.
2. Be wrong.
3. Going somewhere in a car.
6. It's a good pet.
7. Speedily. Rhymes with past.
10. Every. Rhymes with teach.
12. Not all. Rhymes with come.
13. It's for a child. Rhymes with boy.

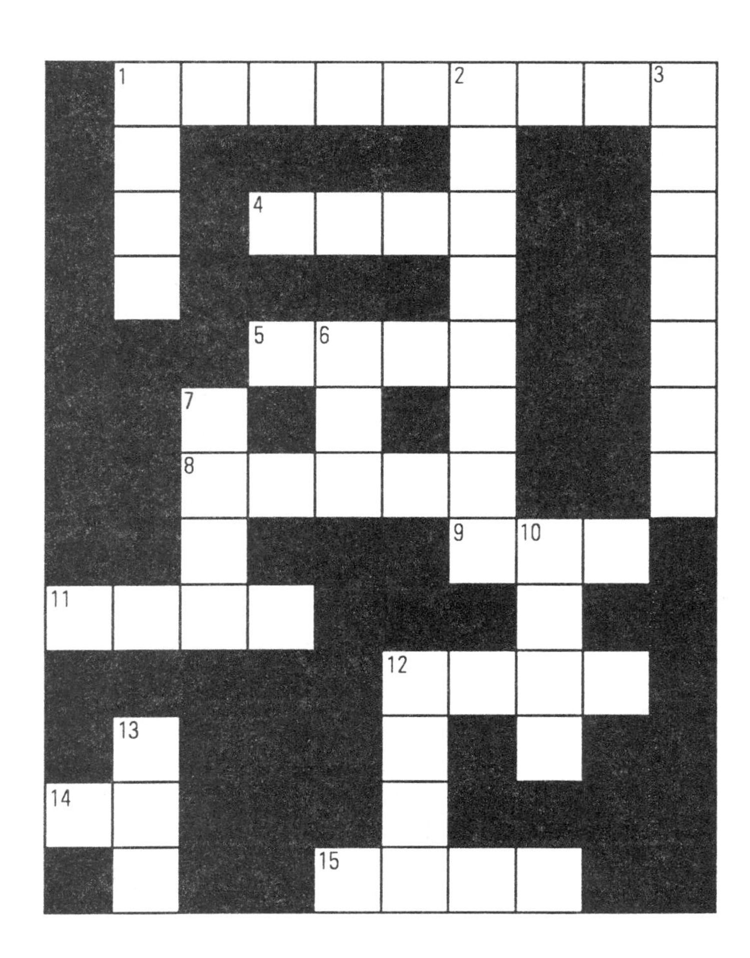

1

2

3

THE DOG IN THE WINDOW

CAST OF CHARACTERS

DADDY
BABY BOY
THE DOG
CHORUS OF UNSOLD DOGS

Dog He likes me,
He likes me,
He wants to take me home.

Chorus He likes you,
He likes you,
He wants to take you home.

Dog That little kid likes dogs, yes,
That little kid likes dogs.

Chorus That little kid likes dogs, yes,
That little kid likes dogs.

Dog He's looking at me,
He's pointing at me.
He wants to take me home.

Chorus He's looking at you,
He's pointing at you.
He wants to take you home.

Baby Boy Buy it, buy it, now, now.
Baby wants it now.

Chorus Now, now.
Buy it, buy it.
Baby wants it now.

Daddy Buy it? Buy what?
What do you want?
I can't understand you,
What do you want?

Baby Boy Baby wants it now,
Baby wants it now.

Daddy Does Baby want a puppy?

Baby Boy Now, now,
Baby wants it now.
Waaaaaaaaaaaaaaaaaa!

Daddy Please stop crying.
I'm trying to understand.

Chorus Baby wants it now.
Baby wants it now.

Daddy I guess he wants that dog in the window.
I guess I'll have to buy a dog.

Chorus Buy a dog, buy a dog,
I guess I'll have to buy a dog.

Daddy If I buy a dog,
I'll have to buy a dog house,
and if I buy a dog,
I'll have to buy a bone.
If I buy a bone,
I'll have to buy a dog bed,
Dog food, dog house, dog bed, bone.

Chorus If he buys a dog,
He'll have to buy a dog house.
If he buys a dog,
He'll have to buy a bone.
If he buys a dog,
He'll have to buy a dog bed,
Dog food, dog house, dog bed, bone.

Daddy Look at the dog, nice dog.
Daddy bought a puppy just for you.

Chorus Look at the dog, nice dog.
Daddy bought a puppy just for you.

Daddy Look at the dog house, nice dog house,
Look at the puppy,
Nice dog.

Chorus Look at the dog house, nice dog house.
Look at the puppy, nice dog.

Baby Boy I don't want a dog house.
I don't want a dog bed.
I don't want a puppy.
I don't want a dog.

Chorus He doesn't want a dog house.
He doesn't want a dog bed.
He doesn't want a puppy.
He doesn't want a dog.

Dog Don't you want a dog?
Don't you want a dog house?
Don't you want to take me home?

Baby Boy NO!

Daddy Look at the dog, nice dog.
Don't you want to take him home?

Baby Boy NO!

Chorus He doesn't want to take him home, no.
He doesn't want to take him home.
He doesn't want a dog.
He doesn't want a dog house.
He doesn't want to take him home.

Daddy You don't want the dog?
What DO you want?

Baby Boy I want a beach ball, beach ball, beach ball.

Chorus Baby wants a beach ball, beach ball, beach ball.
Baby doesn't want a dog.
Baby wants a ball.

Dog Am I hearing right?
The kid wants a beach ball?
A beach ball instead of a dog?

Chorus He wants a beach ball.
He wants a beach ball.
Baby wants a beach ball
instead of a dog.

Dog Now he wants a beach ball.
The kid wants a beach ball.
That little kid hates dogs.

Chorus Now he wants a beach ball.
The kid wants a beach ball.
That little kid hates dogs.

Dog That stupid kid wants a beach ball.
A beach ball instead of a dog!

Chorus That kid wants a beach ball,
A beach ball instead of a dog.

Dog Stupid kid, stupid kid!
A beach ball instead of a dog!

Chorus Stupid kid, stupid kid,
A beach ball instead of a dog!

Dog I'm more fun than a beach ball.
A beach ball is not like a dog.

Chorus We're more fun than beach balls.
Beach balls aren't like dogs.

Dog A beach ball won't bring you the paper.

Chorus Beach balls aren't like dogs.

Dog You can't make friends with a beach ball.

Chorus Beach balls aren't like dogs.

Dog You'll be sorry, Baby.
We could have been good friends.
You'll be sorry someday.
Today our friendship ends.

Chorus You'll be sorry, Baby.
We could have been good friends.
You'll be sorry someday.
Today our friendship ends.

THE DOG IN THE WINDOW

Exercises

Ask Your Partner

A. Ask your partner the following questions and check the answers in the space provided.

		Yes	No
1.	Would you like to work in a pet shop?	☐	☐
2.	Do you think a bird is a nice pet?	☐	☐
3.	Do you have a dog?	☐	☐
4.	Is a bird as intelligent as a dog?	☐	☐
5.	Do they have pet shops in your country?	☐	☐
6.	Would you like to have a talking bird?	☐	☐
7.	Have you ever been bitten by a dog?	☐	☐
8.	Do you think a big dog can be happy in a small apartment?	☐	☐
9.	Do you believe that crying helps you get what you want?	☐	☐
10.	When you were a child did you cry when you wanted something?	☐	☐

B. Write your own answers to questions 1-10 using a short response followed by a complete sentence.
Example: Do you have a pet? Yes, I do. I have a dog.

1. ______________________. ______________________.
2. ______________________. ______________________.
3. ______________________. ______________________.
4. ______________________. ______________________.
5. ______________________. ______________________.
6. ______________________. ______________________.
7. ______________________. ______________________.
8. ______________________. ______________________.
9. ______________________. ______________________.
10. ______________________. ______________________.

Word Puzzle

Use the clues to write the answers.

1. ______________
   a. It starts with "f."
   b. It has 4 letters.
   c. It's the opposite of slow.
2. ______________
   a. It starts with "r."
   b. It has 4 letters.
   c. It rhymes with pain.
3. ______________
   a. It starts with "i."
   b. It has 11 letters.
   c. It is the opposite of boring.
4. ______________
   a. It starts with "e."
   b. It has 3 letters.
   c. It rhymes with send.
5. ______________
   a. It starts with "n."
   b. It has 3 letters.
   c. It's the opposite of old.
6. ______________
   a. It starts with "d."
   b. It has 4 letters.
   c. It's the opposite of up.

Using your answers from the puzzle above, what word do their first letters spell? ______________________

Words And Expressions

A man's best friend is his dog.
Old friends are best.
Good friends are everything.
A friend in need is a friend indeed.

Word Search

How many words can you find?

In the puzzle below, find words from the story and circle them. Some go across, others go down.
Work with a partner. How many other words can you find that are not in the story? List all the words you can find on a separate piece of paper, and add others you need to make one long, correct sentence in English. Who can write the longest sentence? Who can write the funniest? Who can write the shortest?

B O N E B E A C H

A N E W U N S R O

B E D S Y D A Y U

A L O O K S W O S

L O G R N W A L E

L W F R I E N D S

L B O Y C S T O E

A L I K E T O W L

M Y T U R N N E L

1

2

3

FALLING IN LOVE

CAST OF CHARACTERS

VENUS, Goddess of Love
ADONIS, Her lover
CHORUS OF LOVERS

Adonis Every day, the same old thing,
A man, a woman
and a wedding ring.
He loves her, she loves him,
Every day the same old thing.

Chorus Every day, the same old thing,
A man, a woman and a wedding ring.

Venus Cupid shoots his arrow at *him,*
He falls in love with *her.*
Cupid shoots his arrow at *her,*
She falls in love with *him.*

Chorus Same old thing,
Same old thing,
He loves her,
She loves him.

Adonis Why can't we do something else for a change?

Venus How about "He loves her but she doesn't love him"?

Adonis That's not interesting either.

Venus How about "He loves her but she loves his brother"?

Adonis Ah, that's better.
Hey, I have an idea.

Venus What?

Adonis What about this?
"She's falling madly in love with him but he's in love with her mother."

Venus HA! HA! Very funny, but it won't work.

Adonis Why not?

Venus Don't be silly. Let's ask Cupid. He might have a good idea.

Adonis Cupid? A good idea?
He hasn't had a good idea
since the day he was born.
Cupid is stupid.

Chorus Cupid is stupid,
Cupid is stupid.

Venus He's only a baby,
He's doing his best.

Adonis But he can't shoot straight.
His arrows never hit the right person.
He usually misses by a mile.

Venus Don't be hard on Cupid.
He's doing the best he can.

Chorus He's doing the best he can.
He's doing the best he can.
Don't be hard on Cupid.
He's doing the best he can.

Adonis Look, let's watch.
He's going to the park.
It's a beautiful day.
The birds are singing.
The sun is shining.
There's a couple on a park bench.
Let's watch.

Venus Look. He's getting ready. He's pointing at the woman.
She's sitting right there. He can't possibly miss.

Adonis That's what YOU think.

Venus Come on, Cupid! Let's get it right!
Come on, Cupid!

Adonis Come on, stupid!
Let's get it right this time.

Chorus Let's get it right!
Let's get it right!
Let's get it right this time.

Venus Look, he did it.
Right in the heart.
Good for you, Cupid!
You did it right this time.

Venus Look at her.
She's starting to fall.
She's starting to fall in love!

Chorus Look! Look! She's starting to fall.
She's starting to fall in love.

Venus Look at her face.
She's falling in love.
Look at her eyes,
They're shining.

Chorus Look at her face.
She's falling in love.
Look at her eyes,
They're shining.

Adonis You did it once.
Now do it again.
You got the woman.
Now get the man.

Venus UH OH, he made a mistake.
He got the wrong man.

Adonis I knew this would happen.
He did it again.
He got the wrong man.

Chorus The wrong man,
He did it again.
He got the wrong man.

Venus There they go,
Same old thing,
A man, a woman and a wedding ring.

Adonis There they go,
Same old tale,
A man, a woman and a wedding veil.

FALLING IN LOVE
Exercises

Ask Your Partner

A. Ask your partner the following questions and check the answers in the space provided.

	Yes	No
1. Do you fall in love easily?	☐	☐
2. Do you think that true love is difficult to find?	☐	☐
3. Do you know a lot of happy couples?	☐	☐
4. Have you ever fallen in love at first sight?	☐	☐
5. Do you think it is possible to be in love with two people at the same time?	☐	☐
6. How old were you when you first fell in love?	☐	☐
7. Do you believe that true love lasts forever?	☐	☐
8. Do you like romantic movies?	☐	☐
9. Do couples hold hands in public in your country?	☐	☐
10. Do couples kiss in public in your country?	☐	☐

B. Write your own answers to questions 1-10 using a short response followed by a complete sentence.
Example: Do you like love stories? Yes, I do. I like reading love stories.

1. ______________________. ______________________.
2. ______________________. ______________________.
3. ______________________. ______________________.
4. ______________________. ______________________.
5. ______________________. ______________________.
6. ______________________. ______________________.
7. ______________________. ______________________.
8. ______________________. ______________________.
9. ______________________. ______________________.
10. ______________________. ______________________.

Pronunciation Practice

Cupid is stupid,
Cupid's not smart.
He shoots his sweet arrows
At somebody's heart.
He speeds through the air
And he seldom shoots straight.
He leaves lovers speechless.
His power is great.

Words And Expressions

Love is blind	You don't see anything bad about someone you love.
Love makes the world go round	Love is the most important thing in the world.
To fall for To be crazy about To be mad about To be head over heels in love with To have a crush on	To fall in love with
To be seeing someone (she's seeing him)	To have a serious romantic relationship
To have an affair with someone	To be romantically involved
They're just friends	A friendship without romance
A one-night stand	A relationship lasting only for one night

Word Search

How many words can you find?

In the puzzle below, find words from the story and circle them. Some go across, others go down.

Work with a partner. How many other words can you find that are not in the story? List all the words you can find on a separate piece of paper, and add others you need to make one long, correct sentence in English. Who can write the longest sentence? Who can write the funniest? Who can write the shortest?

G	O	O	D	G	L	I	N	S
O	N	C	E	O	L	D	A	Y
D	C	D	I	D	E	A	R	E
D	H	I	T	A	L	E	R	T
E	Y	S	H	O	O	T	O	H
S	L	I	E	S	N	O	W	E
S	A	L	R	I	N	G	R	A
H	P	L	O	V	E	O	U	R

1

2

3

4

THE THING

CAST OF CHARACTERS

CAVE MAN
CAVE WOMAN
FRIEND
CHORUS

Cave Man I can't do it, darn it!
I just can't do it.

Chorus He can't do it, darn it!
He just can't do it.

Cave Woman What's the matter?
What's wrong?
What are you trying to do?

Chorus What's the matter? What's wrong?
What are you trying to do?

Cave Man I'm trying to pick some apples.
Look at that tree.
Plenty of beautiful apples
for you and me.

Friend What about me?

Cave Man There are plenty of apples for three.
Look at the beautiful apples.
Look at the beautiful tree.
But I can't do it, darn it,
It makes me mad.
Look at that fruit,
That's too bad.

Chorus That's too bad, that's too bad,
Look at those apples,
It makes him mad.

Friend Look at that fruit,
Look at that tree,
Plenty of apples
for you and me.

Cave Man Think, think,
What can we do?

Cave Woman Why don't you stand on your toes?

Chorus Stand on your toes,
Stand on your toes,
Why don't you stand on your toes?

Cave Man I tried that. It didn't work.
I stood on my toes,
It didn't work.

Chorus He tried that,
It didn't work.
He stood on his toes,
but it didn't work.

Friend Why don't you try climbing the tree?
Why don't you climb the tree?

Cave Man I tried that.
It didn't work.
I can't climb the tree.

Chorus He tried that,
It didn't work.
He can't climb the tree.

Friend Stretch your arms as far as you can.
Stand on your toes and stretch.

Cave Man It just won't work.
I can't reach the apples
no matter how hard I try.
The tree is too high.

I can't reach the apples
no matter how hard I try.

Chorus It just won't work.
He can't reach the apples
no matter how hard he tries.
The tree is too high.
He can't reach the apples
no matter how hard he tries.

Cave Woman Think, let's think,
Why don't we stop and think?
Why don't we all sit down for awhile?
Why don't we stop and think?

Friend Hey, I have an idea.
Why don't you stand on a rock?

Cave Man Why don't YOU stand on a rock?
That's the worst idea I've ever heard.

Cave Woman Hey, I have an idea.
Let's make a thing to stand on,
A long thing to stand on.

Chorus A long thing,
A long thing.

Cave Man What kind of a thing?

Cave Woman A long thing,
A strong thing to stand on.

Chorus A strong thing to stand on,
A long, strong thing.

Friend The thing will have to be strong.

Cave Man How will we make this thing?

Cave Woman First we'll cut some poles,
long, strong poles.

Cave Man How many poles?

Cave Woman Two poles,
Two long poles.

Cave Man How long?

Cave Woman Very long.

Cave Man Longer than this?

Cave Woman Longer than that.

Friend Longer than this?

Cave Woman Longer than that.
A little bit longer than that.

Cave Man Longer than this?

Cave Woman Longer than that.
A little bit longer than that.

Friend Longer than that?

Cave Woman A little bit longer than that.

Chorus Longer than this?
Longer than that.
A little bit longer than that.

Friend Then what?
Then what?

Cave Woman Then we cut some short poles.

Cave Man How many short poles?

Cave Woman Five strong short poles.

Friend How short?

Cave Woman Very short.

Cave Man Shorter than this?

Cave Woman Shorter than that.
A little bit shorter than that.

Cave Man Now what?
Now what?
The poles are ready.
Now what?

Friend What do we do with the short poles?

Cave Woman We tie them to the long poles.

Chorus Short poles,
Strong poles,
Tie them to the long poles.
Short poles,
Strong poles,
Five short poles.

Cave Man Now what?
Now what?

Cave Woman Is everything ready?

Cave Man Everything's ready.

Friend Wait a minute.
What shall we call it?

Cave Woman Let's call it a ladder.

Friend A ladder?
That's nice.

Cave Woman You two grab the ends.
I'll stand in the middle.
I'll stand on the short poles.
I'll stand in the middle.

Cave Man Like this?

Cave Woman That's right.

Friend Like this?

Cave Woman That's right.
That's right.
Hold tight,
Hold tight,
and lift me up slowly.

Chorus That's right.
Hold tight!
Hold tight!
Hold tight!
That's right!
That's right!
Lift her up slowly.

Cave Woman Higher, higher,
hold tight, hold tight.

Chorus Hold tight, hold tight.
Higher, higher.

Cave Woman There! We did it!
The apples are ours!
The apples are ours!

Cave Man and **Friend** LOOK! We did it!
Hooray for us, hooray!

Chorus LOOK! You did it!
Hooray for you, hooray!
The apples are yours,
The apples are yours.
Hooray for you!
Hooray!

Unit Thirteen

THE THING

Exercises

Ask Your Partner

A. Ask your partner the following questions and check the answers in the space provided.

	Yes	No
1. Do you like apples?	☐	☐
2. Do you know how to make apple pie?	☐	☐
3. Have you ever picked an apple from a tree?	☐	☐
4. When you were a child did you like to climb trees?	☐	☐
5. Have you ever fallen off of a ladder?	☐	☐
6. Do you believe it is bad luck to walk under a ladder?	☐	☐
7. Are there apple trees in your country?	☐	☐
8. Are apples expensive in your country?	☐	☐
9. When you have a problem, do you usually ask your friends to help you find an answer?	☐	☐
10. What is the best season for apple picking?		

B. Write your own answers to questions 1-9 using a short response followed by a complete sentence.
Example: Have you ever made an apple pie? No, I haven't. I have never made an apple pie.

1. ____________________. ____________________.
2. ____________________. ____________________.
3. ____________________. ____________________.
4. ____________________. ____________________.
5. ____________________. ____________________.
6. ____________________. ____________________.
7. ____________________. ____________________.
8. ____________________. ____________________.
9. ____________________. ____________________.

Pronunciation Practice

Apples on a tree
One, two, three
Papa picked an apple
from the old apple tree

Mama took the apple
made a little pie
She never made another one
She wouldn't tell me why.

Climb Up the Ladder

Climb up the ladder
  Slowly carefully

I'll hold the ladder
  Carefully, carefully

Climb down the ladder
  Slowly, carefully

Don't fall off the ladder
  Please!

Hold on to the ladder
  Carefully, carefully

Climb down the ladder,
  slowly, carefully

I'll hold the ladder
  carefully, carefully

Never walk under a ladder
  Please!

Words And Expressions

Two heads are better than one.	People working together can solve problems.
Too many cooks spoil the broth.	Too many people spoil the work.
An apple a day keeps the doctor away.	A popular health tip
A bad apple, a rotten apple (he's a bad apple)	A bad person
As American as apple pie	Typically American
Apple cheeks	Rosy cheeks
It's like comparing apples and oranges.	It's as different as apples and oranges. You can't compare those two things.
Don't upset the applecart.	Don't spoil the plans.

Crossword Puzzle

Work with a partner. The words for this crossword puzzle are from Units Eleven, Twelve and Thirteen. Look at the clues below and fill in the blanks. For each clue, begin in the box with the same number.

Across

1. They wiggle in your socks. Rhymes with rose.
4. Not out.
5. Incorrect. Rhymes with song.
9. Rhymes with stronger.
10. Extremely, much. Rhymes with berry.
12. The first half of one of baby's first words. Or is it the second half? A little word for mother.
13. (2 words). A cave man's wife.
16. Rhymes with so.
17. A long way up. Opposite of low.
19. Rhymes with had.
21. The last part. Opposite of beginning.
22. Travel fast. Rhymes with sun.
23. One of these every day keeps the doctor away. It tastes good.
24. Wish for, need.

Down

1. A cave man never wears one.
2. At the highest place. Opposite of off.
3. Unintelligent. Rhymes with Billy.
5. You look through it. When the door is locked, you climb in.
6. Not a pair. Rhymes with fun.
7. What the green light says. Rhymes with low.
8. It's next to the ocean. Rhymes with peach.
11. Male. Rhymes with fan.
14. It covers your face. Rhymes with pail.
15. Center. Rhymes with fiddle.
16. Above. Opposite of under.
18. Aid, assist. You call for it when you're in trouble.
20. A child's word for father.
23. Rhymes with cat. Not a long word.

ANSWER KEY

Unit One, The Talking Watchdog

Word Search

A	H	O	M	E	B	S	G	W
S	T	E	A	K	U	H	E	H
V	N	T	B	I	R	D	T	A
W	I	H	U	S	G	W	S	T
I	C	A	N	F	L	O	O	R
N	E	T	C	H	A	T	C	G
D	O	G	H	M	R	H	K	O
O	O	T	H	E	L	E	S	O
W	M	A	K	E	F	R	B	D

Across: HOME, STEAK, BIRD, FLOOR, DOG, MAKE

Down: BURGLAR, SH, GET, WHAT, NICE, THAT, BUNCH, SOCKS, WINDOW, GOOD, OTHER

Unit Two, The Fortune Teller and the Bellhop

Word Puzzle

1. Ship
2. Ice
3. Light
4. Van
5. End
6. Rose

The word is SILVER

Word Search

H	E	H	E	A	V	Y	F	A
A	T	C	A	R	E	F	U	L
N	S	O	R	E	R	O	L	U
D	I	D	R	M	Y	R	L	G
A	L	L	I	B	E	B	A	G
L	V	A	N	E	S	A	N	A
O	E	D	G	S	T	L	D	G
C	R	Y	S	T	A	L	I	E
B	Y	L	A	I	R	S	H	E

Across: HE, HEAVY, CAREFUL, DID, MY, BAG, CRYSTAL

Down: HAND, EARRINGS, VERY, FULL, LUGGAGE, SILVER, BEST, BALLS, AND

Unit Three, Everybody's Having A Wondferul Time, Except Me

Word Puzzle

1. Hat
2. Aunt
3. Pie
4. Pepper
5. Year

The word is HAPPY

Crossword Puzzle

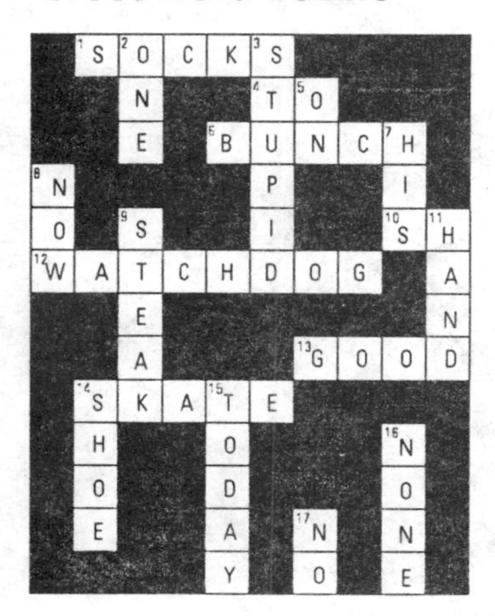

Unit Four, Big Fish, Little Fish

Word Search

R	S	M	A	L	L	G	O	T
S	O	M	E	T	H	I	N	G
O	C	A	U	G	H	T	B	F
T	K	U	M	U	C	H	I	I
D	O	L	L	A	R	N	G	S
P	R	O	B	A	B	L	Y	H
T	W	O	I	H	E	A	V	Y
L	I	T	T	L	E	O	N	E
E	L	S	E	F	I	V	E	N

Across: SMALL, GOT, SOMETHING, CAUGHT, MUCH, DOLLAR, PROBABLY, TWO, HEAVY, LITTLE, ONE, ELSE, FIVE

Down: SOCK, BIG, FISH, BITE

Unit Five, Scared Of The Dark

Word Puzzle

1. Sweet
2. Candy
3. Apple
4. Right
5. End
6. Dark

The word is SCARED

Word Search

L	I	N	O	V	E	R	S	O
A	N	O	S	N	A	K	E	S
S	I	L	L	Y	T	B	E	C
D	R	U	E	W	S	O	F	O
R	O	B	E	A	R	S	O	U
E	M	A	P	T	S	U	R	T
A	E	F	S	C	A	R	E	D
M	A	M	A	H	F	E	S	O
S	T	H	E	R	E	I	T	O

Across: IN, OVER, SO, NO, SNAKES, SILLY, BE, BEARS, SCARED, MAMA, THERE, IT

Down: IN, EATS, SEE, WATCH, SLEEP, FOREST, SCOUT, DREAMS, SURE, DO, MEAT, SAFE

Unit Six, The Rain Dance

Word Puzzle

1. Down
2. Always
3. Nice
4. Clean
5. Empty

The word is DANCE

Crossword Puzzle

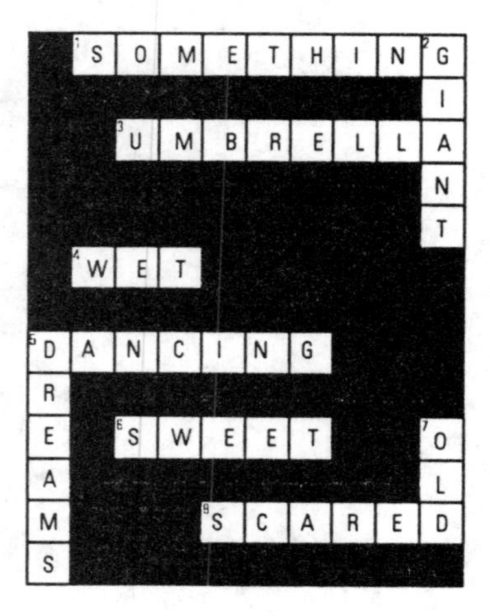

Unit Seven, Toys

Word Puzzle

1. Toy
2. Rain
3. Ask
4. Into
5. Near

The word is TRAIN

Word Search

N	W	A	T	C	H	I	N	G
E	I	N	V	T	R	A	I	N
W	D	A	R	R	I	V	E	L
S	E	E	H	A	P	P	Y	I
H	A	V	E	C	R	N	C	T
D	B	A	C	K	P	S	E	T
R	A	I	L	R	O	A	D	L
I	O	S	W	S	E	T	V	E
P	L	A	Y	T	O	Y	S	R

Across: WATCHING, TRAIN, ARRIVE, SEE, HAPPY, HAVE, BACK, SET, TV, PLAY, TOYS

Down: NEWS, TV, IDEA, TRACK, LITTLE

Unit Eight, Lies

Word Puzzle

1. Save
2. Inch
3. Car
4. Kind

The word is SICK

Word Search

T C R Y I N G I H
H M E D I C I N E
E C A L L O V A L
R O D M O N E Y D
E W S A S I C K W
W H A T E N T S A
H Y D T E N D O N
O L I E S L O S T
T O W R O N G O T

Across: CRYING, MEDICINE, ALL, MONEY, SICK, WHAT, LIES, LOST, WRONG, GOT

Down: HERE, MATTER, WHY, SAD, WANT, WHO, DO, SO

Unit Nine, Madame Rosa And The California Bear

Word Puzzle

1. Door
2. Age
3. Red
4. Keep

The word is DARK

Word Search

N O F U T U R E X
W C O M I N G S B
H L R I G H T L I
A T T A C K B I G
T R U W O W E F R
L B N A U H A E E
X O E L G E R P A
T E L L E R F N T
L U N C H E R E F

Across: NO, FUTURE, COMING, RIGHT, ATTACK, BIG, TELLER, LUNCH, HERE

Down: FORTUNE, WHAT, LIFE, GREAT, WALL, WHERE

Unit Ten, The Traffic Ticket

Word Puzzle

1. Slow
2. Park
3. Easy
4. End
5. Drive

The word is SPEED

Crossword Puzzle

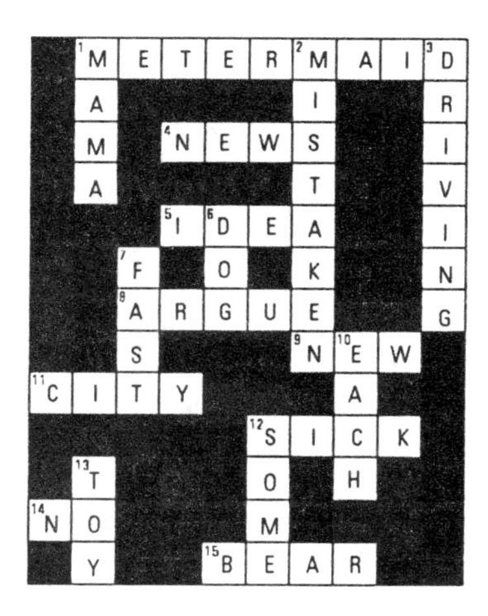

Unit Eleven, The Dog In The Window

Word Puzzle

1. East
2. Rain
3. Ice
4. End
5. New
6. Down

The word is FRIEND

Word Search

B	O	N	E	B	E	A	C	H
A	N	E	W	U	N	S	R	O
B	E	D	S	Y	D	A	Y	U
A	L	O	O	K	S	W	O	S
L	O	G	R	N	W	A	L	E
L	W	F	R	I	E	N	D	S
L	B	O	Y	C	S	T	O	E
A	L	I	K	E	T	O	W	L
M	Y	T	U	R	N	N	E	L

Across: BONE, BEACH, BED, DAY, LOOK, FRIENDS, BOY, LIKE

Down: BUY, ENDS, CRY, HOUSE, BALL, DOG, SORRY, WANT, NICE, WE

Unit Twelve, Falling In Love

Word Search

G	O	O	D	G	L	I	N	S
O	N	C	E	O	L	D	A	Y
D	C	D	I	D	E	A	R	E
D	H	I	T	A	L	E	R	T
E	Y	S	H	O	O	T	O	H
S	L	I	E	S	N	O	W	E
S	A	L	R	I	N	G	R	A
H	P	L	O	V	E	O	U	R
E	E	Y	E	S	Y	T	L	T

Across: GOOD, ONCE, OLD, DAY, IDEA, ARE, HIT, TALE, SHOOT, OH, NOW, RING, LOVE, EYES

Down: GODDESS, GOD, ARROW, EITHER, SILLY, HEART, GOT

Unit Thirteen, The Thing

Crossword Puzzle

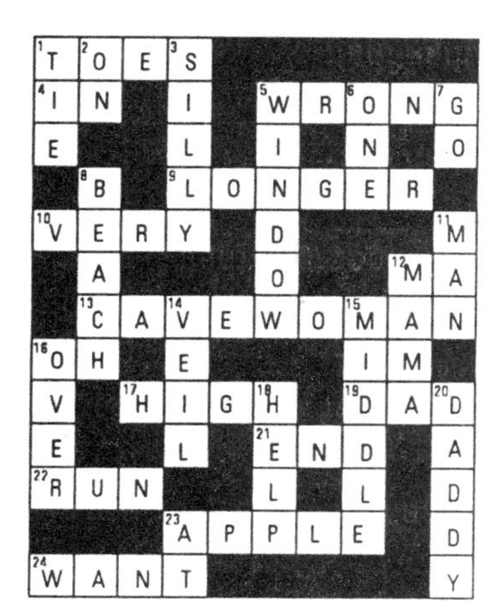